KU-637-596

Also by Barbara Hannay:

MOLLY COOPER'S DREAM DATE
A MIRACLE FOR HIS SECRET SON
EXECUTIVE: EXPECTING TINY TWINS
THE CATTLEMAN'S ADOPTED FAMILY
EXPECTING MIRACLE TWINS
THE BRIDESMAID'S BABY
HER CATTLEMAN BOSS

I wish to remember those who suffered the devastation of the Queensland floods in January 2011.

Many homes and lives were lost in the very places where this story is set.

CHAPTER ONE

IT BEGAN on an everyday, average Monday morning. Zoe arrived at the office punctually at eight forty-five, clutching her takeaway coffee, a necessary comfort when facing the start of the working week. To her surprise, her best friend Bella was already at work.

Bella was usually a bit late, and as she'd just spent another weekend away visiting her father in the country Zoe had expected her to be later than ever. This Monday morning, however, Bella was not only at her desk *early*, but she had a huge grin on her face. *And* she was surrounded by a semicircle of excited workmates.

She was holding out her hand as if she was showing off a new manicure. No big surprise. Bella had a thing for manicures and she often chose very out-there nail polish with an interesting assortment of decorative additions.

But as Zoe drew closer, curious to check out her friend's latest fashion statement, she saw that Bella's nails were painted a subdued and tasteful taupe. And they were *not* the focus of everyone's attention.

The grins and squeals were for a sparkling ring.

On Bella's left hand.

Zoe's cardboard coffee cup almost slipped from her

suddenly weak grasp. She managed to catch it just in time.

She was stunned.

And a bit stung, too.

Struggling to hang on to her smile, she hastily dumped the coffee and her handbag on her desk and hurried over to Bella.

She told herself she was misreading this. Bella couldn't be engaged. Her best friend would most definitely have told her if wedding bells were in the air. Zoe knew for a fact that Bella wasn't even dating anyone at the moment. Together, they'd been commiserating about their date drought, and they'd talked about trying for a double date online.

They'd even considered going on an overseas holiday together—a reconnaissance tour, checking out guys in other countries. Deepening the gene pool, Bella had called it during one of their regular Friday nights together.

Admittedly, for the past three weekends in a row Bella had travelled to her country home on the Darling Downs, and Zoe had been beginning to wonder what the attraction was. Bella had said she was worried about her widowed father, which was totally understandable, as her dad had been in a miserable slump for the past eighteen months ever since her mum died.

Bella had also mentioned her close and supportive neighbours, the Rigbys, and their son, Kent—literally, the boy next door, whom she'd known all her life.

Was something going on with this guy? Had he given Bella this ring?

Bella hadn't breathed a *hint* about a romance with anyone, but it was abundantly clear that the sparkle on her friend's finger was most definitely a diamond. And the name on her lips was…

'Kent Rigby.'

Bella was grinning directly at Zoe now, an expectant light shining in her pretty green eyes.

'Wow!' Zoe managed, squeezing her cheek muscles to make sure she was smiling and not still looking like a stunned mullet. 'You're engaged!'

Bella dipped her head ever so slightly, as if she was trying to read Zoe's reaction, and Zoe cranked her smile another notch while she hunted for the right things to say. 'So—does this mean you and the boy next door have taken the plunge after all?'

She was trying not to sound too surprised, and she *hoped* she looked happy. She certainly didn't want the entire office to realise she was totally clueless about her best friend's romance.

Just in time, she remembered to give Bella a hug, and then she paid due homage to her ring—a solitaire diamond, very tasteful, in a platinum setting, and appropriately delicate for Bella's slim, pale hands.

'It's gorgeous,' Zoe told Bella with genuine honesty. 'It's perfect.'

'Must have cost a bomb,' commented one of the girls behind her in an awed voice.

Eric Bodwin, their boss, arrived then and an awkward hush fell over the office until someone piped up with Bella's happy news.

Eric frowned, dragging his bushy eyebrows low, as if an employee's impending marriage was a huge inconvenience. But then he managed to say 'Congratulations,' with a grunting nod in Bella's direction, before he disappeared into his private den.

He'd never been the type of boss who chatted with

his staff, so everyone was used to his gruffness. Nevertheless, his dampening presence put an end to the morning's excitement.

The semicircle of onlookers melted away. Only Zoe remained, her head so brimming with a thousand questions she was reluctant to go back to her desk. And she couldn't help feeling a tad put out that Bella had never confided in her.

'Are you all right, Zoe?' Bella asked cautiously.

'Of course, I'm fine.' Zoe touched Bella's ring finger. 'I'm stoked about this.'

'But you didn't reply to my text.'

'What text?'

'The one I sent you last night. Just before I left Willara Downs, I texted you with my good news.'

'Oh?' Zoe pulled a sheepish face. 'Sorry, Bell. I took myself to the movies last night, and I turned my phone off. Then I forgot to switch it back on.'

'Must have been a good movie,' Bella said dryly, but she was smiling again.

'It was. A lovely, mushy romance.'

Bella rolled her eyes, but they grinned at each other and Zoe was ridiculously pleased that she hadn't been left out after all.

'Meet me at The Hot Spot at lunchtime?' Bella asked next.

'Absolutely.' The busy little café on the corner was their favourite, and a meeting today was top priority.

Back at her desk, however, Zoe's spirits took another dive as she came to grips with the reality of Bella's startling news. She was losing her best friend. Bella would move back to the country to live with Kent Rigby and that would be the end of her close friendship—their mutual support over office grumbles, their lunchtime chats, their Friday night cocktails and joint shopping sprees.

It was definitely the end of their overseas holiday plans. And it was very puzzling that Bella had never confided in her about Kent. What did that say about their supposedly close friendship?

Glumly, Zoe retrieved her phone from her handbag and flicked it on to find two unread messages—both from Bella.

At 6.35 p.m. last night:

The most amazing thing! Kent and I are engaged. So much to tell you. B xx

And then at 9.00 p.m.:

Where r u? Gotta talk. x

Zoe winced. If she'd been available for a heart-to-heart chat last night, she'd know everything now and perhaps she'd understand how this engagement had happened so quickly.

Instead, she had to get through an entire morning's work before she received a single answer to her thousand and one questions.

'You're getting *married*?'

'Sure.' Kent pitchforked fresh hay into the horse stall, then angled a meaningful glance to his mate Steve who leaned on the rails, watching. 'Why else would I be asking you to be my best man?'

Steve's eyes widened. 'So you're dead-set serious?'

'I'm serious.' Kent grinned. 'Getting married isn't something to joke about.'

'I guess it isn't. It's just that we all thought—' Steve stopped and grimaced.

'You all thought I'd carry on playing the field for ever,' Kent supplied.

'Maybe not for ever.' Steve's grin was sly. 'But heck man, you never gave the impression you were planning to settle down just yet, even though plenty of girls have tried their hardest.'

Kent's jaw tightened as he thrust the pitchfork back into the hay bale. He'd anticipated Steve's surprise— and yeah, maybe his disbelief—but his friend's reaction still rankled. It was true that he'd dated plenty of girls without getting serious. In the past. But those days were over now. He had responsibilities to shoulder.

Steve's ruddy face twisted into a baffled smile, and he scratched at the side of his sunburned neck. 'Crikey.'

'You're supposed to say congratulations.'

'Of course, mate. Goes without saying.' Balancing a booted foot on the rail, Steve leaned into the stall, holding out his hand. His eyes blazed with goodwill. 'Congratulations, Kent. I mean it. Bella's an ace girl. She's terrific. The two of you will be a great team.'

He shook Kent's hand.

'Thanks.'

'I shouldn't have been so surprised,' Steve added, accompanying the words with a shrug. 'It makes sense. You and Bella have always been like—' He held up a hand, displaying his index finger and forefinger entwined.

Kent acknowledged this truth with a nod and a smile. He and Bella Shaw had been born six months apart to families on neighbouring properties. As infants they'd shared a playpen. As youngsters they had joint swimming and riding lessons. They'd gone to school together, travelling into Willara each day on the rattling school bus, swapping the contents of their lunch boxes and sharing the answers to their homework.

From as far back as Kent could remember, their two families had gathered on the banks of Willara Creek for regular barbecues. Their fathers had helped each other with shearing or mustering. Their mothers had swapped recipes, knitting patterns and old wives' tales.

When Kent was just six years old, Bella's dad had saved his life…

And now, with luck, Kent was returning the favour.

He felt OK about it. Honestly, he was happy with the future he and Bella had planned.

Just the same, Kent would have been relieved to get a few things off his chest to Steve. In the past few years his load had mounted steadily.

When his dad had hankered for an early retirement, Kent had taken on the bulk of the farm work. Then Bella's mother had died, and her father, the very man who'd saved his life when he was a kid, had started drinking himself to death. Desperately worried, Kent had helped out there as well, putting in long hours ploughing fields and mending neglected fences.

Bella, of course, had been distraught. She'd lost her mother and now she was likely to lose her father, and if these weren't enough troubles to bear, her family's property was rapidly going down the drain.

A host of heavy emotions was tied up in their decision to marry, but although Kent was tempted to confide in Steve he wouldn't off-load his baggage, not even to his best friend.

'I hear Bella's dad's in a bad way,' Steve said. 'He's been keeping very much to himself and he needs to slow down on his drinking.'

Kent's head shot up. Had Steve guessed things were worse than most people realised?

'Tom has the beginnings of heart failure,' he said slowly.

'That's a worry.'

'It is, but if he looks after himself, he should be OK.'

Steve nodded. 'And once you're his son-in-law, you'll be able to keep a closer eye on him.'

Clearly, Steve thought their decision was reasonable, but then his eyes flashed as he sent Kent a cheeky smirk. 'You and Bella are a sly pair though, keeping this under wraps in a gossipy town like Willara.' He snapped a piece of straw between his fingers and raised his eyebrows. 'So, when's the happy day? I suppose I'll have to wear a penguin suit.'

When Zoe burst into The Hot Spot, Bella was already there, waiting in their favourite corner booth with salad sandwiches and two chai lattes.

'That was the longest morning of my life,' Zoe moaned as she hurled herself into a seat. 'Thanks for getting lunch.'

'It was my turn.'

Reaching across the table, Zoe touched the diamond on Bella's left hand. 'This is real, isn't it? You're properly engaged. I'm not dreaming.'

'It's totally real.' Bella gave a crooked little grin. 'But I must admit I still have to pinch myself.'

'You, too?' Drawing a deep breath to calm her racing thoughts, Zoe asked carefully, 'So...you weren't expecting this engagement?'

'Not really,' Bella said, blushing. 'But it wasn't exactly a surprise either.'

Zoe blinked and gave a helpless flap of her hands.

'I'm sorry, I'm lost already. You're going to have to explain this.' She took a sip of her chai latte, but she was too intent on Bella's response to register the sweet and spicy flavour she usually loved.

'There's not a lot to explain.' Bella tucked a shiny strand of smooth blond hair behind one ear. 'The thing is…even when we were kids there was a lingering suggestion from Kent's and my parents that we might eventually—you know—end up together some day. They teased us when we were little, then toned it down later, but all the time we were growing up it was there in the background as a possibility.'

This was news to Zoe and she couldn't help asking, 'How come you've never mentioned it?'

Bella looked contrite. 'You must think I'm crazy, talking so much about guys without ever really mentioning Kent.'

'You spoke about him, but you said he was just a friend.'

'He was. For ages. We were just…neighbours…and good mates…' Her shoulders lifted in a casual shrug. 'To be honest, I'd never seriously thought about marrying him. But then—'

Zoe leaned closer. 'Is Kent the reason you've headed for home every weekend lately?'

Pink crept into Bella's cheeks and her green eyes took on a touching mistiness as she held out her left hand and admired her ring again. 'It sort of crept up on us. Kent's been so sweet.'

'Oh-h-h…' Watching the dewy smile on Bella's lips, Zoe was overcome by the romantic possibilities of her friend's situation. Her skin turned to goose bumps and she could picture it all: a wonderful, long-term friendship where a couple felt really comfortable with each other, and knew each other inside out—all the good bits and the bad. Then, suddenly, they were hit by a blinding and beautiful truth.

So different from Zoe's soul-destroying experience with Rodney the Rat.

'Out of the blue you just realised you were in love and meant for each other,' she said.

Bella nodded.

'And you definitely know Kent's Mr Right?'

Another nod.

Zoe couldn't believe the way her throat was choking up. 'I thought those blinding flashes of insight only happened in movies, but look at you. This is a real life friends-to-lovers romance!' To her embarrassment, a tear spilled down her cheek.

'So you understand?' Bella's smile was a mixture of sympathy and relief.

'My head's still trying to catch up, but I guess I understand here.' Not caring how melodramatic she looked, Zoe pressed a hand over her heart. 'I'm happy for you, Bell. Truly.'

'Thanks.' In a blink, Bella was out of her chair and the girls were hugging. 'I knew you'd understand.'

'Your dad must be thrilled,' Zoe said when Bella had sat down again.

To her surprise, a flood of colour rushed into Bella's face and then she paled and looked down at the sandwich in front of her. She pulled at a piece of lettuce poking out from the bread. 'Yes, he's very happy,' she said quietly.

Puzzled, and just a little worried by the reaction, Zoe wasn't sure what to say next. Something wasn't right here.

Or was she imagining Bella's tension?

She wondered if Bella's dad had expressed mixed feelings. It would be bittersweet for Mr Shaw to watch his daughter's engagement blossom so soon after his wife's death. He'd miss having her there to share the joy with him.

Zoe thought about her own parents, settled at last, running their little music shop in Sugar Bay and raising her little brother, Toby. After Toby's unexpected arrival when Zoe was fourteen, her mum and dad had undergone a dramatic transformation. By the time she'd started work and Toby was ready for school, they'd given up their nomadic existence, travelling round the country in a second-rate rock band.

But becoming conventional parents hadn't dimmed their love for one another. They'd remained fixed in a crazy love-struck-teenager groove and, although their relationship had always left Zoe feeling on the outside, she couldn't imagine either of them having to manage alone. Not for ages, at any rate.

Poor Mr Shaw…

'Earth to Zoe. Are you there?'

Zoe blinked, and realised Bella had been talking, and by the look of frustration on her face she'd been saying something important. 'Sorry. I—ah—missed what you said.'

Bella sighed and gave a little, heaven-help-me eye roll. 'I said I was hoping you'd be my bridesmaid.'

Zap!

Zoe's heart gave a jolt, like a soldier jumping to attention. She'd been so busy getting her head around Bella's new status as fiancée, she'd given no thought to her actual wedding. But bridesmaid?

Wow!

She had a sudden vision of Bella looking lovely in

white, with a misty veil…and herself in a beautiful bridesmaid's gown…

There'd be bouquets…and handsome guys in formal suits…

She'd never been a bridesmaid.

Warmth flooded her and she felt quite dizzy with excitement. 'I'd love to be your bridesmaid. I'd be totally honoured.'

This was no exaggeration. In fact, Zoe was quite sure Bella could never guess how over-the-top excited she was about this.

She'd heard other girls groan about being bridesmaids. They seemed to look on the honour as a boring chore and they told war stories about having to wear horrible satin gowns in the worst possible colours and styles.

Talk about ungrateful! For Zoe, being a bridesmaid was a wonderful privilege. She would wear anything Bella chose—puce coloured lace or slime-toned velvet—she wouldn't care. Being Bella's bridesmaid was clear, indisputable evidence that she was someone's really close friend.

Finally.

Oh, cringe. Anyone would think she was a total loser.

Well…truth was…she'd actually felt like a loser for much of her childhood. She'd had so few chances to make close friends, because her parents had dragged her all around the country, living—honest to God—in the back of a bus. There'd never been time for her friendships to get off the ground.

Her best effort had been in the fifth grade when the band broke up for a bit and her parents had stayed in Shepparton for almost twelve months. Zoe had become really good friends with Melanie Trotter. But then the band had regrouped and her parents had moved on, and the girls' letter exchange had lasted six months before slowing to a trickle, then, inevitably, dried up.

It wasn't until Zoe started work at Bodwin & North and met Bella that she'd finally had the chance to form the kind of ongoing friendship she'd always longed for. And now, here was the proof—an invitation to be Bella's bridesmaid.

Zoe beamed at Bella. 'Will it be a country wedding?'

'Yes—on the Rigbys' property—Willara Downs.'

'Wow. That sounds utterly perfect.' Ever since her childhood, travelling through endless country towns, Zoe had known a secret yearning to drive through a farm gateway instead of whizzing past. Now, she wouldn't merely be driving through the farm gate, she'd be totally involved in the proceedings.

Wow, again. She could picture Bella's big day so easily—white-covered trestle tables on a homestead veranda. A ceremony beneath an archway of pale pink roses. Male guests with broad shoulders and suntans. Women in pearls.

'So...how many bridesmaids are you planning' She tried to sound casual, which wasn't easy when she was holding her breath. Would she be sharing this honour with six bridesmaids? Hadn't she read somewhere that a celebrity had eighteen attendants—all of them in purple silk?

'Only one,' Bella said calmly as she spooned fragrant froth from the inside of her glass. 'It won't be a big flashy wedding. Just family and close friends. I've never wanted a swarm of bridesmaids.' She smiled. 'I just want you, Zoes. You'll be perfect.'

Perfect. What a wonderful word.

'I'll do everything I can to make the day perfect for *you*,' Zoe said.

There was no question—she would try her utmost to be the *perfect* bridesmaid. She would research her duties and carry them out conscientiously. No bride had ever had a more dedicated wedding attendant. 'So, do we have a date? Is there a time line?'

'Actually, we were thinking about October twenty-first.'

'Gosh, that's only a few weeks away.'

'I know, but Kent and I didn't want to wait.'

How romantic.

Zoe supposed she'd hear the phrase *Kent and I* rather a lot in the next few weeks. She wondered, as she had many times, what it was like to be so deeply in love.

But then another thought struck. Leaning closer, she whispered, 'Bell, you're not pregnant, are you?'

'No, of course not.'

'Just checking, seeing you're in such a rush, in case my bridesmaid's duties involved knitting bootees.'

Bright red in the face, Bella slapped her wrist. 'Shut up, idiot.'

'Sorry.' Zoe smiled. 'Well, a tight deadline can focus the mind wonderfully.'

'It shouldn't be too hard to organise. Everything will happen at the homestead, so we won't need to book a church, or cars or a reception venue, and the local rector is a good friend of the Rigbys.'

'So you only have to buy a wedding dress and order a cake.'

'Yes. Too easy,' Bella said with a laugh, and then as they started on their sandwiches her face grew more serious. 'I've made an appointment with Eric Bodwin. I'll have to resign, because I'll be living at Willara, but

I was also hoping we might be able to arrange time off
for you as well, so you can come out and help with all
the last minute organising. I don't want to burden Kent
with too much of the legwork. But I know the time off
would eat into your holiday allowance—'

'That's fine,' Zoe said quickly. 'I'd love a week or
so in the country.' She was feeling a bit down at the
thought of Bella resigning, but then she grinned. 'As a
bonus, I might have a chance to wangle a nice country
romance of my own.'

Bella's eyes danced. 'Now that's a thought.'

It wasn't just an idle thought for Zoe. As a young girl,
experiencing constant brief tastes of country towns before moving on, she'd developed something of a penchant for the jeans-clad sons of farmers with their
muscular shoulders and rolling, loose-hipped strides.

'Mind you,' Bella said, 'I've grown away from country life since I moved to Brisbane.'

'But you're looking forward to going back and settling down as a farmer's wife, aren't you?'

Bella gave her lower lip a slightly troubled chew. 'It
will certainly be an adjustment.'

'I think it sounds idyllic,' Zoe said honestly. 'But then
I probably have a romanticised idea of life on a farm.
I've never actually been on one.'

'Why don't you come home with me next weekend?' Bella suggested with a sudden beaming smile.
'We could go together after work on Friday. It only takes
a little over an hour. You can meet Kent and I can show
you where we're planning to have the wedding, and you
can help me to nut out the details.'

'Wow. That sounds wonderful.'

'Actually, you know how hopeless I am at organising. I'll probably hand you pen and paper and a list of phone numbers for caterers.'

'That's OK.' No doubt it was pathetic, but Zoe loved to feel needed. 'I'd love to come. Are you sure there's room for me to stay?'

'Of course I'm sure. We won't stay with my dad. He hasn't been well and he'd get in a stew about clean sheets and things. We can stay at Willara Downs. The homestead is huge and Kent's a wonderful host. His parents live in town these days, but they'll probably come out and you can meet them, too. They'll welcome you with open arms.'

Again Zoe thought of all the times her parents had whizzed in and out of country towns when she'd longed to stay. She'd been constantly looking in from the outside, never really getting to know the locals.

Now, for a short time, for the *first* time, she would be an insider.

'I'd love that. We can take my car,' she offered, eager to help any way she could. 'It's so much easier than getting the bus.'

Already, in her head, she was compiling a list of her bridesmaid's responsibilities. Number one—she would support Bella and help her to stay calm through the next nerve-wrangling weeks. Perhaps she would also help her to address the wedding invitations, and then there would be a hen night to arrange…and a bridal shower…

It was going to be fabulous. She was determined to carry out every task to the very best of her ability. Her aim was nothing less than perfection.

CHAPTER TWO

THE next weekend, fifteen kilometres from Willara Downs, Zoe heard an unmistakable flap, flap, flap coming from her car's rear tyre. Her stomach took a dive. *Not now. Please, no!*

But it was useless to hope. She'd heard that flapping sound too many times in her childhood—her dad had always been changing flat tyres on their bus. Now she knew with sickening certainty that she had no choice but to pull over onto the grassy verge and try to remember what to do.

It wasn't fun to be alone, though, on the edge of an unknown country road at dusk on a Friday evening. Zoe wished she hadn't been so convincing when she'd assured Bella she'd be fine to drive on to Willara Downs by herself, while Bella visited her dad.

Two days ago, Bella's father had been admitted to hospital. Apparently, Kent Rigby had found Mr Shaw in a very bad state and insisted on rushing him in to Willara.

Understandably, Bella had been beside herself with anxiety and Zoe had dropped her in town.

'Kent's not answering his phone, so he's probably out on the farm, but he'll understand if you turn up alone,' Bella had assured her.

'And one of us will come back to pick you up in an hour or so,' Zoe suggested.

'Yes, that will be great.'

And so…after expressing the wish that Mr Shaw was much improved, Zoe had set off happily enough—at least she was driving her own car and she felt at ease behind the wheel. And apart from concern about Mr Shaw's illness, she was dead excited about this weekend away and getting to meet Bella's fiancé… seeing the wedding venue…being part of the planning.

The very last thing she needed was a flat tyre.

Damn.

Briefly, Zoe toyed with the idea of trying the Willara Downs number to see if Kent Rigby could help. But it was such a bad way to start the weekend, to be seen as a useless city chick who wouldn't even *try* to fix a simple problem by herself.

Resigned, she climbed out. The tyre was as flat as a burst balloon, and she went to her boot to hunt for the jack and the thingamabob that loosened the wheel nuts.

Mosquitoes buzzed as she hunted. The jack was, of course, buried under all the luggage—two overnight bags, two make-up bags, two sets of hot rollers.

'You never know, there *might* be a party,' Bella had said.

Now, with their belongings scattered haphazardly on the side of the road, Zoe squatted beside the wheel, positioned the jack and got on with turning its handle.

So far so good…except she didn't really know how high she was supposed to raise the car. And once that was done…she wasn't certain she was strong enough to loosen the wheel nuts. They looked mighty tight. And even if she did get them off, would she be able to tighten them up again?

Zoe's unhelpfully vivid imagination threw up a picture of her car driving off with the back wheel spinning free and bouncing into the bush, while she struggled with an out-of-control steering wheel.

Maybe she *should* try to ring for help.

Standing again, she reached into the car for her handbag. As usual, because she really needed it, her phone had slipped from its handy side pouch to the very bottom of her bag, so she had to feel around among movie tickets, keys, lipsticks, pens, old shopping lists, tissues…

She was still fumbling when she heard the sound of a vehicle approaching. Her spirits lifted. This *might* be nice, friendly country folk only too happy to stop and help her.

The thought was barely formed, however, before Zoe felt a shaft of hot panic. If only she hadn't watched all those horror movies. Here she was—totally alone in the silent, empty bush wondering if the driver was an axe murderer, an escaped prisoner, a rapist.

She made a final, frantic fumble in the bottom of her bag, and her fingers closed around her phone just as a white utility vehicle shot around the curve.

There was only one person in the ute and all she could see was a black silhouette, distinctly masculine. He was slowing down.

Zoe's nervous heart gave a sickening thud as his ute came to a complete stop and he leaned out, one strong, suntanned forearm resting casually on the window's rim.

In panic, she depressed the call button on her phone and glanced quickly at the screen.

No signal. She was out of the network. *Oh, terrific.* There was no hope of a rescue.

'Need a hand?' the driver called.

At least he had a friendly voice—mellow and warm with a hint of good humour.

Zoe gulped, and forced herself to look at him properly. She saw dark, neatly trimmed hair and dark eyes. Not threatening eyes, but genial, friendly, and framed by a handsome face. Nicely proportioned nose, strong jaw and a generous mouth.

Already his door was swinging open, and he stepped out.

He was wearing a crisp blue shirt with long sleeves rolled back from his wrists and pale cream moleskin trousers. His elastic sided riding boots were tan and well polished. Zoe had always fancied that look—clean cut with a hint of cowboy. Surely, an axe murderer wouldn't go to so much trouble?

'I see you've got a flat,' he said, coming towards her with the easy loose gait of a man of the land. 'That's rotten luck.'

He smiled and his eyes were deep, coffee-brown— friendly eyes, with a spark of fun, and with laughter lines fanning from the corners.

In spite of her fears, Zoe couldn't help smiling back at him. 'I've just about got the car jacked up, but I wasn't sure how far I should take it.'

'I'd say you have it just right. The perfect height.'

Perfect. It was fast becoming one of her favourite words.

Suddenly, she couldn't remember why she'd been scared of this fellow. There was something about his smile and about his face that was incredibly, importantly *right*.

In fact…Zoe felt as if a gong had been struck deep inside her, and it took a magnificent effort to force her attention away from this stranger to her problem. 'I was—um—about to tackle the wheel nuts.'

'Would you like a hand with them?' He was smiling again and her skin tingled deliciously. 'If that doesn't offend you.'

'Why would I be offended by an offer of help?' *From a gorgeous man*, she added silently.

He shrugged. 'Thought you might be like my little sister—the independent type. She hates it when guys assume she needs help when she doesn't.'

'Oh, I see.' The mention of his sister relaxed Zoe even further. Actually, she was so relaxed she was practically floating, and she offered him a radiant smile. 'I'd love to say I could manage this tyre on my own, but, to be honest, I'm really not sure I *can* manage. I was just about to phone for help.'

'No need. It won't take long.'

'That's awfully kind of you.' Holding out the wheel thingamajig, she hoped her saviour didn't get grease on his clothes.

Clearly not sharing her concern for his pristine trousers, he hunkered down beside the wheel and began working smoothly and efficiently.

Nice hands, Zoe noticed. He was nice all over, actually. Tall and muscular. Not too lean, not too beefy. She suppressed a little sigh, and told herself she was a fool to feel fluttery over the first country fellow she met. Before this wedding was over she'd meet tons of cute rural guys.

But there was something special about this man, something totally entrancing about the warmth in his brown eyes and the quirk of his smile, a subtle *something* that made her heart dance and her insides shimmy.

Strange she could feel so much when all his attention was focused on her car's rear wheel.

'Now for the spare.' Having loosened the wheel, he was standing up again, and he glanced Zoe's way.

Their gazes linked and…

He went very still. And a new kind of intensity came into his eyes. He stared at Zoe…as if he'd had a shock, a pleasant, yet deeply disturbing shock.

Trapped in his gaze, she could feel her face glowing hot as a bonfire, and she was struck by the weirdest sense that she and this helpful stranger were both experiencing the same awesome rush. Deep tremors—happy and scary at once—as if they had been connected on an invisible wavelength.

This can't be what I think it is.

Back to earth, Zoe.

She realised that the stranger was frowning now and looking upset. Or was he angry? It was hard to tell. His brow was deeply furrowed and he dropped his gaze to the ground and his throat worked as he stared at a dried mud puddle.

Zoe held her breath, unable to speak or even think, and yet incredibly aware that something beyond the ordinary had happened.

Then her rescuer blinked and shook his head, as if he was ridding himself of an unwanted thought. He cleared his throat. 'Ah—the spare tyre. I guess it's in the boot?'

Turning away from Zoe, he made his way to the back of the car, skilfully stepping between the scattered pieces of luggage.

'I'm sorry,' Zoe spluttered, struggling to shake off the unsettling spell that seemed to have gripped her. 'I should have fetched the spare tyre and had it ready for you.'

'No worries.' He spoke casually enough, but when he looked back at her he still seemed upset, as if she'd done something wrong. But then, without warning, he smiled.

His smile was warm and friendly again, and once more Zoe was electrified. Instantly. Ridiculously. She found herself conjuring a picture of him in a farmhouse kitchen, smiling that same yummy smile across the breakfast table at her, after a night of delicious love-making.

Good grief. Next minute she'd be imagining him naked.

Could he guess?

'Excuse me.'

His voice roused her. Blushing, she stepped out of his way as he carried the new wheel and hefted it into position. But, heaven help her, she was mesmerised by the strength of his shoulders and the sureness of his hands as he lined up the wheel as if it weighed no more than a cardboard button, and fitted it into place.

'You've done this before,' she said.

'So many times, I could do it in my sleep.'

Zoe wasn't sure it was wise to let her mind wander in the direction of this man's sleep. Better to keep the talk flowing.

She said, 'I've watched my dad change tyres on country roads enough times. I should have picked up a few more clues.'

He looked up at her, clearly surprised. 'Which country roads? You're not from around here, are you?'

'No. My parents were in a band and they toured all around the various country shows.' She hoped any resentment she felt for those nomadic gypsy years hadn't crept into her voice.

'Which band?' he asked, pausing in the middle of tightening a nut.

'Lead the Way.'

'You're joking.'

Laughing, Zoe shook her head. 'No, I'm afraid I'm serious.'

'Were both your parents in Lead the Way?'

'Yep. My dad was the lead singer and my mum was on drums.'

'So you're Mick Weston's daughter?'

'His one and only.' It wasn't an admission Zoe needed to make very often. Since she'd started work in the city she'd hardly met anyone who'd heard of her parents or their band.

'Amazing.' To her surprise, he threw his head back and laughed. 'Wait till I tell my old man. He's a huge fan of Mick Weston. Never missed a Lead the Way performance in Willara.'

Fancy that. Zoe beamed at him. It was heartening to be reminded that her dad had been very popular out here.

But, heavens, now she and this stranger had something in common and she found herself liking him more than was sensible. Perhaps encouraging conversation wasn't such a bright idea.

She busied herself with securing the punctured tyre in the boot and restowing all the bits and pieces of luggage.

By the time she'd finished, her good Samaritan was removing the jack. 'That's done,' he said, straightening and dusting off his hands.

'Thank you so much. It's incredibly kind of you. I

really am very grateful.' *And just a little sad that we'll have to say goodbye now...*

He stood with his feet apart, hands resting lightly on his hips, watching her with an enigmatic smile. 'What about you?' he asked. 'Do you sing or play the guitar?'

''Fraid not.' Zoe returned his smile—seemed her face was permanently set in smile mode. 'The musical genes totally bypassed me.'

'But you inherited your dad's talent for flat tyres on country roads.'

'Yes…unfortunately.'

Wow. Instead of rushing off, he was making conversation with her. And Zoe loved it. She was no longer bothered that he was a stranger. She was too busy enjoying this amazing experience—the most awesome sensation of being swept high and pumped full of excitement, as if she were riding a magnificent, shining wave.

Were her feet still touching the ground?

She'd never felt like this before. Not with a complete stranger. Not with this bursting-from-a-geyser intensity. Rodney the Rat didn't count. He'd been a work colleague and she'd known him for twelve months before he asked her out.

Truth was—Zoe usually lacked confidence around guys. She guessed it was part of an overall lack of confidence, a problem that stemmed from her childhood when she'd always been the new girl in town, always arriving late in the term when all the friendship groups were firmly established. She'd grown up knowing she'd never quite fitted in.

But this man's gorgeous smile made her feel fabulously confident and suddenly her biggest fear was that he would simply drive away—out of her life.

'I'll tell my dad I met the son of one of his fans,' she told him.

'Do you have far to go?' her helper asked.

'I don't think it's much farther. I'm heading for Willara Downs.'

He stiffened. 'Willara Downs?'

'It's a property near here—a farm.'

'Yes, I know.' Now, he was frowning again. 'It's my property.'

His property?

Really?

A sudden chill swept over Zoe. He wasn't…

He couldn't be…

'You're—you're not—a Rigby, are you?'

'I certainly am.' He smiled, but it was a shade too late, and with only a fraction of its former warmth. 'The name's Kent Rigby.' His smile wavered as he asked uncertainly, 'Should I know you?'

Oh, God, he was Bella's Kent…Bella's boy next door.

Kent's been so sweet, Bella had said.

No wonder he was nice. He was the man her best friend was about to marry.

A cool breeze made icy goose bumps on Zoe's skin. The purple tinged dusk crowded in and she felt suddenly, terribly weary. And wary.

'We haven't met,' she said quietly, hoping she didn't sound as ridiculously disappointed as she felt. 'But we'll soon have a lot to do with each other. I'm Zoe. Bella's bridesmaid.'

Kent Rigby's eyes darkened and his features were momentarily distorted, as if he tried to smile but couldn't quite manage it.

But if he'd been caught out, he was very good at covering it up. 'Sorry, I should have guessed,' he said,

speaking smoothly once more, with no hint of distur-
bance. 'But I expected you to be with Bella.'

Calmly, he held out his hand.

Unhappily, she felt the warmth and strength of his
hand enclose hers in a firm clasp. 'Hello, Kent.'

'Hi, Zoe.'

'I dropped Bella off at the hospital. She tried to call
you to explain that I'd be arriving on my own.'

Kent had forgotten to let go of her hand. 'I'm actually on my way back from seeing Tom myself,' he said.

'How—how is he?'

'Slightly improved, thank God.'

Suddenly he realised he was still holding her hand.
Letting go, he cracked a slightly embarrassed grin, then
thrust his hands into his jeans pockets. He straightened
his shoulders, then looked to the sky in the east where
a huge full moon was already poking its golden head
above a dark, newly ploughed field. 'I guess Bella will
ring when she's ready to be picked up.'

'Yes.'

'We'd better get going, then. Would you like to follow me? I'll keep you in my rear vision, so I'll know
you're OK.'

'Thanks.'

As Zoe followed Kent Rigby's ute she tried to laugh
at herself. What a fool she'd been, getting all hot and
bothered about a stranger she'd met on a road side.

Shouldn't she have guessed that a hot-looking guy
like Kent would have already been taken? Hadn't she
learned anything from her experience with Rodney?

OK, so she was feeling ridiculously disappointed
right now, but she'd get over it. She'd been looking forward to this weekend too much to let anything spoil
it. She'd been so excited about Bella's wedding and

being her bridesmaid. She'd wanted to be the *perfect* bridesmaid.

That was still her goal. Having a fan-girly moment over the bridegroom had been a minor hiccup, but she'd recover in no time.

In the fading light of dusk, which just happened to be Zoe's favourite time of day, the track she and Kent were driving along emerged out of a purple-shadowed tunnel of trees onto sweeping lawns, dusky and magical in the twilight.

Zoe saw an archway of rambler roses and a weeping willow...an elegant, Federation-style house, long and low, with lights already glowing on the veranda.

The car's wheels crunched on white gravel as she pulled up behind Kent's ute in front of smooth sandstone steps flanked by garden beds filled with agapanthus and lilies. When Kent got out, she saw him silhouetted against the backdrop of his home. Damn. It was such an attractive image—but she had to stop thinking like that.

She had no choice. This gorgeous man was Bella's future husband and there was no way she would let her silly imagination give into any more reckless fantasies.

'I'll show you to your room,' Kent said with the gracious charm of a perfect host, which showed that he at least knew exactly what *his* role was.

Zoe followed him down a hallway past an elegant lounge room with deep squishy sofas and rich Oriental rugs to a pretty bedroom that was the epitome of comfort and tasteful country-style décor.

With her things stowed, she was taken out to a wisteria-scented back veranda, and soon found herself sitting in a deep cushion-lined cane chair, sipping

chilled white wine while she and Kent looked out in
the fading light to the most beautiful view of fields and
distant hills.

She suppressed an urge to sigh. Everything about
Kent Rigby's home was as gorgeous as he was. And
it was all so beautifully presented she supposed he
must have a housekeeper and a gardener. Lucky Bella
wouldn't be a slave to housework.

As a child, looking out of the bus window, Zoe
had dreamed of living in a lovely farmhouse like the
Rigbys', but she'd never been the jealous type and she
wasn't about to start now.

Very soon Bella would return from the hospital and
take her rightful place at Kent Rigby's side. And Zoe's
silly road side mistake would be a thing of the past.

Clutching an icy glass of beer as if his life depended on
it, Kent struggled to ignore the girl sitting beside him.
Not an easy task when he was her host and hospitable
manners had been ingrained in him from birth.

Problem was, he was badly rattled and he couldn't
really understand how he'd got this way. Anyone would
think he wasn't used to meeting new girls—when the
truth was quite the opposite.

He could only assume the problem arose because he
hadn't adjusted to his newly engaged status. No doubt
that would explain the crazy chemistry that had gripped
him from the moment he set eyes on Bella's bridesmaid.

Why the hell hadn't he introduced himself to Zoe
Weston as soon as he stepped up to help her? If he'd
known who she was, he could have avoided those telling moments—those shocking spellbinding seconds
when he'd felt drawn to her, as if a bizarre spell had
been cast over him.

Chances were, he'd never have noticed her inexplicable appeal, that special *something* in her eyes, and in the sheen of her hair or the tilt of her smile—a quality that rocked his easy-going nature to its very foundations.

How crazy was that? He'd exchanged nothing more than a few glances with her.

Kent knew it was nothing more than an illusion. A mistake. It was more than likely that every man experienced a similar difficulty in his pre-wedding weeks. Commitment to one girl didn't automatically stop a guy from noticing other girls. Learning to ignore their appeal was part of the adjustment to being engaged or married.

In Kent's case, his commitment was binding on all kinds of levels, and there was no going back. No regrets. He was a man of his word.

Besides, if he was rational about this, there wasn't even anything particularly special about Zoe Weston. Her brown hair and blue eyes and slim build were nice enough, but her looks were average. Surely?

The imagined attraction was merely a blip, and now he could put it behind him.

That settled, Kent took a deep, reassuring draft of beer, pleased to realise he'd been overreacting.

It wasn't as easy as Zoe had hoped to relax while sitting beside Kent on his veranda. She found herself crossing and uncrossing her legs, fiddling with the stem of her wine glass, or sneaking sideways glances at her host's stare-worthy profile. Hardly the behaviour of a perfect bridesmaid.

Desperate to stop this nonsense, she jumped to her feet and leaned on the veranda railing, looking out at the parklike sweep of gardens that stretched to a timber fence, and fields of golden crops and grazing animals.

Concentrate on the wedding—not the groom.

Casually, she asked, 'Are you planning a garden wedding, Kent?'

He looked surprised, as if the question had caught him out, but he responded readily enough. 'An outdoor ceremony would be great and the weather forecast is promising. What do you think?'

Rising from his chair, he joined her at the veranda's edge, and once again Zoe was struggling to ignore his proximity. Now there was the tantalising whiff of his cologne to deal with as well.

She concentrated on the lawns and banks of shrubbery. 'A garden wedding would be perfect. Would you hire a caterer?'

'That's one of the things we need to discuss this weekend. But Bella's a bit...distracted.'

'Yes, her dad's health is a big worry for her.'

Kent nodded, then let out a heavy sigh.

'You're worried, too,' Zoe said, seeing the sudden tension in his face.

'I have to be careful what I say around Bella, but I'm angry with her dad.' Kent sighed again. 'Don't get me wrong. Tom Shaw's a wonderful guy. In many ways he's been my hero. But his wife died eighteen months ago and he dropped his bundle. He started drinking heavily, and now he has the beginnings of heart failure.'

'From drinking?'

'From drinking and generally not looking after himself.' Kent's hand fisted against the railing. 'Bella's beside herself, of course.'

'I hadn't realised his health was so bad,' Zoe said with concern. 'Poor Bell.'

'Don't worry.' Kent spoke quietly, but with unmistakable determination. 'I'll look after her. And I'm damned if I'll let Tom kill himself.'

Wow, Zoe thought. Kent had sounded so—so *noble*; he really was Bella's knight in shining armour.

And clearly he was happy in that role. He was turning to Zoe now with a smile. 'Bella said you're going to be a great help with the wedding.'

'I—I'm certainly happy to do all I can to help.'

'She claims you're a fabulous organiser and list-maker.'

'I suppose I can be. I've never organised a wedding, but I quite like planning our office Christmas party. A smallish wedding won't be too different.' To Zoe's dismay, her cheeks had grown very hot. She shot a quick glance out to the expanse of lawn. 'I imagine you'd need to hire tables and chairs.'

'Yes, definitely.'

'And table cloths, crockery, glassware et cetera.'

'I dare say.' Kent flashed a gorgeous crooked smile. 'If you keep talking like that you'll land yourself a job, Zoe.'

And if he kept smiling at her like that she wouldn't be able to refuse.

CHAPTER THREE

IT WAS late on Sunday night before the girls arrived back in Brisbane. As Zoe drove they discussed practical matters—the style of wedding gowns and invitations, and the things they needed to hire for the garden reception. They were both tired, however, and, to Zoe's relief, they spent much of the journey in reflective silence.

She dropped Bella off at her flat in Red Hill, declining her invitation to come in for a drink with the excuse that they both had another Monday morning to face in less than ten hours.

'Thanks for spending the weekend with me,' Bella said as she kissed Zoe's cheek. 'And thanks for offering to help Kent with organising the reception. Well, you didn't actually offer, but thanks for agreeing when I pleaded. We all know I can't organise my way out of a paper bag.'

'That's OK,' Zoe responded glibly, hoping that she sounded much calmer than she felt about ongoing communication with Bella's fiancé—even if it was only via email or telephone.

'And thanks for taking your car, Zoe. So much better than bumping along in the old bus.'

'My pleasure.' However, Zoe couldn't possibly share Bella's opinion on this matter. If she hadn't taken her car, she wouldn't have had a flat tyre and she wouldn't have had a private meeting with Kent. And her weekend would have been a darned sight easier.

'Thanks for inviting me, Bell. It was—wonderful. You're going to have the most gorgeous wedding ever.'

'I know. I'm so lucky.' Bella's green eyes took on a wistful shimmer. 'You do like Kent, don't you?'

Zoe's heart took a dive, but she forced a bright smile. 'Of course. What's not to like? He's lovely. Perfect husband material. You should have snapped him up years ago.'

Bella smiled, looking genuinely happy now, as if she'd needed this reassurance. Then she grabbed the straps of her overnight bag, slammed the door and called, 'See you in the morning.'

Zoe watched as Bella hurried up her front steps, pale hair shining in the glow cast by a streetlight, then she drove on, feeling the last of her strength ebb away.

All weekend she'd held herself together—remaining upbeat and excited for Bella's sake, while keeping a lid on her own private turmoil. Dropping any interest in Kent had proved much harder than she'd expected, and now the ordeal was over she was totally drained. She just wanted to crawl into her own little space and let go.

Finally, she reached her flat in Newmarket, let herself into the kitchen, dumped her bag in the corner.

She loved her little home. For the first time in her life she had a proper place to call home that had four walls instead of four wheels.

First she checked her goldfish—Brian, Ezekiel and Orange Juice. They'd survived beautifully without her. Then she dashed out onto her balcony to make sure her pot plants were still alive.

Zoe had always kept pot plants, even when they

were in the bus. Her mum said she'd inherited Granny Weston's green thumb, and Zoe saw it as a sign that she was meant to have her own plot of land.

One day.

Back in the kitchen, she reached for the kettle. First priority was a comforting mug of tea, accompanied by a long soak in a warm bath. She could sort out her laundry tomorrow night after work. For now, she was going to be totally self-indulgent.

Five minutes later, warm, rose-scented water enveloped her, and at last she could set her thoughts free.

Unfortunately, her thoughts zeroed straight to Kent Rigby.

She let out the loud groan she'd been holding in for two whole days, ever since the road-side revelation on Friday evening. All weekend, honest to God, she'd tried unbelievably hard to stop liking Kent.

It should have been easy. He was her best friend's fiancé, and Zoe had already dated a previously engaged man. She'd been burned. Horribly. After she'd dated Rodney for several months and helped him to get over his break-up, he'd moved in with her and she'd been deeply in love with him. Then she'd come home unexpectedly early one evening and found him in bed with Naomi, his former fiancée.

Rodney the Rat.

Never again would Zoe set herself up for that kind of heartache.

So why hadn't she found the 'off' switch for her attraction to Bella's fiancé?

It was ridiculous, as if she'd contracted a mutant strain of a virus that was resistant to all known treatments.

The truth was that deep down she was genuinely

thrilled for Bella. Willara Downs was the lifestyle her
friend had been born into. Bella's parents had always
lived in the district. Her father would soon be out of
hospital and home on his farm, and her grandfather still
lived in an aged care facility in Willara township. On
top of that, the Shaw and Rigby properties were adjoin-
ing and so Bella and Kent had the whole dynasty thing
happening.

Beyond all these practical considerations, Bella and
Kent were so sweet together, and so very at ease. Maybe
they weren't all touchy-feely, but that was to be expected
when others were around. Just the same, it was clear as
daylight that they belonged together.

Without question, Bella fitted in. She'd found where
she belonged, while once again, as always, Zoe was the
outsider.

Oh, God.

Zoe dunked her face under the water to wash away
her stupid tears. She had to get a grip. Had to stop this
nonsense now.

Curse that flat tyre.

This problem would never have arisen if she and
Bella had driven to the homestead together. If Bella
had been there, from the moment Zoe met Kent she
would have known who he was, and the first thing she
would have seen was Kent embracing his bride-to-be.
She would have been excited for Bella, and her heart
would have stayed safely immune to Kent's charms.

Instead, cruel fate had delivered her a punctured tyre
and twenty minutes alone with a wonderful man who'd
arrived like a gift from heaven.

She kept reliving that thrilling moment—only a
few seconds admittedly—when their gazes had con-

nected. She could have sworn something huge and earth-shattering had passed between them.

Had it all been in her stupid head?

She hated to admit that she'd deluded herself, but there was no other explanation. Thank heavens Kent hadn't noticed.

His behaviour had been beyond reproach. He'd been unfailingly polite and friendly to Zoe, and he'd been wonderful about her damaged tyre, organising a replacement to be sent out from a garage in Willara and then fitting it for her.

Appropriately, he'd devoted the bulk of his attention to Bella. There'd been no sign that he was remembering the moment when he and Zoe had looked into each other's eyes and the world had stopped.

And she was going to be just as sensible.

It was time for self-discipline and maturity. Time to get a grip on reality.

Kent-slash-man-of-her-dreams-Rigby was going to marry her best friend in less than two months and she, Zoe Weston, was going to be their happy, loyal, non-jealous, and perfect-in-every-way bridesmaid.

Kent couldn't breathe. Pinned at the bottom of a dark muddy pool, he could feel his lungs bursting, his legs thrashing. He couldn't see a thing. Couldn't hear anything either, just a dull roaring in his head.

Fear, blacker than the night, pressed down with a weighty and smothering hand.

He fought, struggling, gasping…shooting awake out of a tangle of sheets.

He dragged in air. His heart raced, but he wasn't panicking. He knew it would slow down soon. He was used to this dream. He knew its familiar pattern, even though he had no real memories of almost drowning in Willara Creek.

The dreams were based on what his family had told him—that he'd been pinned under a rock and Tom Shaw had saved him, and that little Bella had been there, white-faced and sobbing.

Don't let Kent die. Please, please don't let him die...

It was years later, in his teens, that the dreams had begun. By then it had finally sunk in that all life was tenuous and that Kent's own life had nearly ended when he was six years old.

A kid showing off. All over red rover. Then a man with good instincts diving down and dragging him free.

Tom Shaw had given Kent a second chance at life, and with that gift had come responsibility.

The dreams never let Kent forget. He owed. Big time.

To: Kent Rigby<willaraKR@hismail.com>
From: Zoe Weston<zoe.weston@flowermail.com>
Subject: Caterers etc.
Dear Kent,
Thanks for your kind hospitality on the weekend. It was great meeting you and having the chance to see where the wedding will take place.

I'm sure you'll be pleased to hear that my spare car tyre held up splendidly, so thanks for your help with that as well.

As you know, I had a good chat with your mother about the best caterers to approach for the wedding and I've rung them all and am sending you their quotes as an attachment for your perusal.

I showed the quotes to Bella, but she has enough to think about with finding her dress and worrying about her dad and she's more than happy to leave the planning details to us.

I thought the menu supplied by Greenslades sounded delicious and it also provides a range of dishes to suit most tastes, but they're a little more expensive than the others.

I'm also sending a link to a website with the table settings that Bella and I think will be perfect. If you like them, I'll go ahead and place an order.

Oh, and are you still happy to use the homestead verandas if there's a threat of rain, or would you like me to look into hiring a marquee?

If there's anything else I can do to help, please let me know.

Kind regards,

Zoe Weston

To: Zoe Weston<zoe.weston@flowermail.com>
From: Kent Rigby<willaraKR@hismail.com>
Subject: Re: Caterers etc.

Hi Zoe,

Thanks for your email with the quotes and the link. Has it occurred to you that you may have missed your calling as a wedding planner?

I agree that the Greenslades menu is a standout, so let's go with them, especially as they're based in Toowoomba and they can send out a mobile kitchen. Great find.

The table settings look terrific—I'm happy to go with whatever you girls choose.

Zoe, you might be Bella's best friend, but I think

you've just become mine, too. Such a load off my mind to have this sorted so quickly and easily.

Cheers

Kent

P.S. I was wondering—do you have a favourite colour?

To: Kent Rigby<willaraKR@hismail.com>
From: Zoe Weston<zoe.weston@flowermail.com>
Subject: Re: Caterers etc.

Dear Kent,

All the bookings are made and both Greenslades and the Perfect Day hire company will be sending you their invoices with details about deposits etc.

Ouch. I hope you don't get too much of a shock.

I'm leaving the ordering of drinks to you. Bella and I will look after the flower arrangements and decorations. So now the major details are planned, but I'd also like to have a bridal shower and a hens' party for Bella, so there's a bit more to be sorted. I guess you and your best man will be having a bucks' night?

As Bella has probably told you, she's found a dress she loves, so it looks as if everything is coming together.

I can't imagine why you want to know my favourite colour. I'm not even sure I can answer that question. It depends if you're talking about a colour to wear, or a colour to look at. It can make quite a difference, you know.

Regards,

Zoe

To: Zoe Weston<zoe.weston@flowermail.com>
From: Kent Rigby<willaraKR@hismail.com>
Subject: Re: Caterers etc.
Hi Zoe,
Once again, thanks for all your help. I can't imagine how this wedding could have happened without you.

As for the question about your favourite colour, I'm afraid I can't really explain. It's a small but pleasant task Bella has assigned to me.

That's a fascinating observation you've made about colours. For now, could you give me both your favourite colour to wear and your favourite colour to look at?
Cheers
Kent

On the following Saturday morning, Bella bought her wedding dress. Zoe had been with her when she'd first seen the dress on the previous Saturday, and they'd loved it. Twice during the week Bella had been back to the shop to look at it again, and now she'd dragged Zoe along with her to approve her final decision.

'Each time I see it, I love it more,' Bella had confided, and as Zoe watched her parade across the store's plush carpet she totally understood why. The floor-length gown was very simple, but its elegant lack of fussiness totally suited Bella's blond, country-girl beauty. Its style, with beautifully embroidered straps and Grecian draping, was perfect for an outdoor country wedding.

'Kent will adore you in this,' Zoe said as she pictured Bella coming across the lawn to her waiting bride-groom. 'You'll stop him in his tracks.'

She was proud that she said this with a genuine smile, although putting the Kent nonsense out of her thoughts hadn't been as easy as she'd expected. Emails in which he asked about her favourite colour hadn't helped.

She still hadn't answered that one. It was silly of her, but it felt too...personal.

'This is definitely the dress for me,' Bella said, giving a final twirl to admire her reflection in the full-length mirror.

She paid for her dress with her credit card, then linked her arm through Zoe's. 'OK, it's your turn now. We have to find something really lovely for you.'

Abruptly, in the middle of the salon, Bella stopped. 'Have I told you how incredibly grateful I am for everything you're doing to help? Kent told me how brilliant you've been.'

'I've enjoyed it,' Zoe said honestly. 'So far, it hasn't been a huge job. Really.'

'But it's such a relief to know it's all in hand,' Bella said. 'Since my dad got sick, I've been rather distracted.'

'That's why I was happy to help.'

'You're one in a million. You know that, don't you?'

It was hard not to bask in the warmth of Bella's smile. Zoe found it incredibly reassuring to be appreciated, to feel needed and important.

Businesslike once more, Bella turned to a rack of dresses. 'I thought if we chose something that didn't scream bridesmaid, you'd be able to wear it afterwards. Colour-wise, I was wondering about—'

Bella paused, looking at a row of dresses, and Zoe waited. Even though she hadn't answered Kent's question about colours, she rather liked pink. She knew lots of girls avoided pink like the plague, but she'd always thought the colour brought out the rosy tones in her skin and went rather well with her dark hair. So, she was thinking of a pretty shade of pink when Bella said, 'Green.'

'Green?'

Bella nodded emphatically. 'I can really see you in green, Zoe. It suits you beautifully. And it's so fresh, just right for a country wedding.'

Yes, green was fresh, no doubt about that. But it was also the colour of grass and trees, and there were rather a lot of both in the country. In the outdoors, green would work like camouflage, wouldn't it?

Worse, wasn't green the colour of jealousy? *Oh, cringe.* Zoe had worked extremely hard to rid herself of any jealousy. Even so, *green* was the last colour she wanted to wear to *this* particular wedding.

Bella was frowning at her. 'Don't you like green? I thought you loved it. That long green scarf of yours looks stunning with your black winter coat.'

But I won't be wearing my black winter coat, Zoe wanted to remind her. *We're supposed to be choosing a dress for a spring garden wedding. If not something with a hint of pink, why not a pretty pale primrose?*

Not that Zoe would actually say any of this out loud, not when she was still, in spite of her minor problem re the groom, trying to be the perfect, considerate bridesmaid.

With a pang of guilt, she remembered the Monday morning, almost two weeks ago now, when Bella had asked her to be her bridesmaid. She'd been ready to wear anything then, even a black plastic garbage bag.

Somewhat ashamed, she said, 'I'm sure a pale apple green could be very nice.'

'Hmm.' Bella was looking less certain now. 'I must admit I hardly wear green myself.' Already, she was heading over to a rack of pretty pastels. 'Our high-school uniform was green, so I had an overdose of it in my teenage years.'

'Oh,' Zoe gasped and smacked the side of her fore-head. 'I'd almost forgotten until you mentioned your high school. I had a message on Facebook from one of your old school friends.'

'Really?' Bella was already at a rack, reaching for a coat hanger with a rather pretty pink dress.

'I posted a message on Facebook, you see, about how excited I was to be a bridesmaid at a country wedding near Willara. I didn't actually mention Willara Downs and I didn't give full names, but I said the bride was my best friend, Bella. I hope you don't mind, Bell.'

'No, of course I don't mind. So who was it?'

'A guy. I think he's been living somewhere overseas, but he said he used to know a girl called Bella Shaw at Willara High and he wondered if she was my friend getting married.'

Bella was suddenly very still and she shot Zoe a strangely nervous glance.

'I haven't replied to him,' Zoe said, cautiously.

'What's his name?' Bella's voice was barely above a whisper now.

'I'm trying to remember. I think it might have been David. No, that's not right. Maybe Damon? Yes, I'm pretty sure it was Damon.'

'Damon Cavello?'

'Yes, that's it. I—' Zoe stopped, shocked into silence by the sight of Bella's deathly pale face and the coat hanger slipping from her hands, landing on the bridal salon's white carpet in a sea of frothy pink chiffon.

'Bell?' With a pang of dismay, Zoe bent down to pick up the fallen gown before any of the store's assistants noticed. 'Bella?' she repeated as she slipped the gown's straps onto the hanger and returned it to its rightful place on the rack. 'What's the matter?'

Bella gave a convulsive little shudder, then the colour rushed back into her face. 'Nothing. Nothing's the matter,' she said quickly. 'I just got a surprise. It's so long since I've heard from D-Damon.'

As she stammered his name her cheeks turned deep pink.

'Who is he?' Zoe had to ask. 'A high-school sweetheart?'

With a startled laugh, Bella whipped her gaze back to the rack, and began, rather distractedly, to check out the dresses. 'God, no. We were just friends.'

'Right.' Zoe frowned as she watched Bella's hands, with their smart navy-blue nail polish and sparkling diamond engagement ring, swish along the coat hangers.

Bella turned to her, eyes extra bright. 'When did you say Damon wrote to you?'

'I found his message when I got home from work last night.'

'But you haven't written back to him?'

'Not yet. I thought I'd better check with you first. I wasn't sure he was someone you wanted to know.'

'Of course you can answer him. There's no problem. Damon's—fine.'

Bella sounded calm enough on the surface, but something wasn't right. Zoe could sense her inner tension.

'Damon was always a bit of a daredevil.' Bella spoke a little too casually, as if she needed to prove she was mega cool about this subject. 'He moved back to Brisbane in the middle of his final year, and he went on to study journalism. He's been overseas for years—as a foreign correspondent, specialising in all the worst trouble spots.'

'He sounds like an adventurer.'

Softly, Bella said, 'I hate to think of the things he must have seen.'

Zoe nodded, still puzzled by the tension Bella couldn't quite disguise. 'I think he might be heading back to Australia,' she said. 'Or he could even be on his way already. So is it OK to pass on your email address?'

'Of course.' This time Bella gave an offhand shrug, as if Zoe had been trying to make Mount Everest out of a molehill.

Lifting a very pretty coffee-and-cream floral dress from the rack, she said, 'If Damon's back in Australia, he's bound to come out to Willara. His father doesn't live there any more, but his grandmother's in the same old folks' home as my grandad, and I'm sure he'll want to visit her. They've always been close. His gran shows me all the postcards he sends her.'

'That's nice.'

Bella bit her lip and gave an uncertain smile.

'Would you invite him to the wedding?' Zoe asked.

'Heavens, no.' A strange snorting laugh broke from Bella. 'He wouldn't be interested in my marriage.' Then her eyes met Zoe's and she frowned. 'Don't look at me like that, Zoe. Damon's not the type to enjoy a romantic country wedding.'

'OK. Just asking. I thought he might have been an old friend of Kent's, that's all.'

She heard the hiss of her friend's sharply indrawn breath.

'Well, yes,' Bella admitted, almost reluctantly. 'Kent and Damon were mates at one time, so I suppose I should tell Kent.' She sighed. 'Actually, he'll probably want to include Damon.'

Then, as if deliberately changing the subject, she held out the coffee-toned dress. 'Now, why don't you try this one on? I can see you in it already.'

It was pretty obvious that Bella wanted to drop the subject. 'All right.'

In the changing cubicle, however, Zoe took one look at herself in the pretty bridesmaid's dress, and she forgot about Bella and the old school friend.

The colour was perfect—tawny flowers on a creamy white background that totally flattered her complexion. But her first thought was not to wonder how she looked.

But— *Would Kent like me in this?*

This was getting tedious.

On Tuesday evening, Zoe was in the middle of important, toenail-painting research when the phone rang. She and Bella were wearing toe peepers to the wedding, and each night, following Bella's instructions, Zoe was trying out a different colour. Serious comparisons were made the next day in their lunch hour.

This evening, when the phone rang, Zoe had toe separators in place and three nails painted with rosy minx, so she was grumbling as she screwed the lid on the bottle and hobbled over to the phone. 'Hello?'

'Hi, Zoe.'

The caller was male with a smooth as molasses country drawl that she instantly recognised. Her heart tried to leap clear out of her chest.

He said, 'Kent Rigby here.'

Why was he ringing? Several scenarios flashed before Zoe. All of them impossible. *Good grief. Calm down.* He'd be ringing about another planning detail.

But when she tried to speak, she sounded distinctly breathless.

'Zoe, are you OK?' Kent sounded genuinely concerned.

'I'm perfectly fine,' she managed to insist, although it came out in a choked whisper. 'Just a bit puffed. I had to—' *quick breath* '—come running in from outside.'

Great. Now she could add dishonesty to her list of sins. Grimacing, Zoe willed herself to calm down. Developing high blood pressure before the wedding was not on the bridesmaids' list of duties.

She took another breath, deeper and slower, aiming for a tone that was friendly, but as businesslike as possible. 'What can I do for you, Kent?'

'I wondered if you've made a decision about the hens' night. I hear you're in charge of that, too.'

'Oh, right, do you want an invitation?' she teased.

Kent chuckled at her weak joke. 'My best man, Steve, has been pressuring me about a bucks' night, and I didn't want it to clash with your arrangements.'

'Actually, I sent you an email about it earlier this evening.'

'Sorry. I haven't checked my emails. I've been out on the tractor since the early hours and I just got back. Thought I'd give you a quick call while my dinner's heating up.'

Zoe pictured Kent up before dawn, out ploughing the fields as the sun rose. Farmers worked such long hours. She wondered if Bella would be the sort of wife who took her farmer husband a Thermos of coffee and a snack. Maybe they'd share a quick cuddle behind the machinery shed?

Oh, God. Stop it!

Assuming her briskest, most businesslike voice, she said, 'We'd like to have the hens' night in Willara, on the weekend before the wedding—that's the same weekend as the bridal shower. Bella's friends from Brisbane don't mind trekking off to the wilds of the country for two weekends in a row, but I think three would be expecting too much.'

'Fair enough.'

'So the girls are planning to book into the Willara pub—that is, unless you want to have your bucks' night there.'

'No, you stay with that arrangement. We'll have the bucks' party on the same night, but we'll go over to Mullinjim. It's not far out of town.'

'Great. That sounds like a plan.' Zoe let out a nervous, huffing laugh. 'So it looks like the wedding's all coming together?'

'Like clockwork. Piece of cake, thanks to you, Zoe.'

A small silence fell and Zoe was shocked to hear her heartbeats, still galloping away like a cattle stampede. She would rather keep talking than risk Kent hearing them, so she asked the question that had been on her mind for days.

'Has Bella mentioned Damon Cavello, the old school friend who made contact?'

'No,' Kent said slowly. 'She hasn't.'

There was no mistaking the surprise in his voice. A beat later, he asked, 'So...what's the wild boy up to these days?'

Zoe could quite believe why Kent had called Damon a wild boy. She'd checked out photos of him on the internet and he had the dark, scruffy, bad-boy looks of a rock-and-roll star. It wasn't a look that appealed to her—

she'd seen enough of guys like that hanging around her parents' band while she was growing up—but she knew bad boys were considered very sexy by girls confident enough to attract them.

'Damon's on his way back to Australia,' she told Kent. 'Coming from Afghanistan, I think.'

Another small silence.

'Is he OK?' Kent asked.

'As far as I know, he's fine.'

'That's a miracle.' Kent spoke with uncharacteristic cynicism, but then he quickly corrected himself. 'Don't get me wrong. I'm relieved to hear that he's in one piece. But with Damon, there's always a risk of—' He left the sentence dangling. 'Do you know if he's likely to be around for the wedding?'

'I think there's a good chance.' Zoe hoped she wasn't breaching Bella's confidence. But then, because she was curious, she couldn't help adding, 'He sounds rather mysterious.'

'Yeah.' There was a barely concealed sigh on the other end of the phone line. 'He's always been a bit of a puzzle, but Bella knew what drove him better than any of us. What did she tell you?'

'Not much at all—just that he left Willara High in Year Twelve and ended up becoming a foreign correspondent. I got the impression he's attracted to danger.'

'No doubt about that,' he muttered.

She could hear definite tension in Kent's voice now, the same tight caution she'd sensed in Bella. What was it about this Damon guy that put everyone on high alert?

'How did Bella react to the news?' Kent asked carefully.

This last question was a curly one. Zoe sensed she was on dangerous ground, and, no matter what she thought of Kent, her loyalty lay with Bella. She certainly wouldn't tell him that Bella had been rather edgy and strange when she'd heard about Damon Cavello.

'Bella said—ah—that she'd talk to you to see if you wanted to invite him to the wedding.'

'But she didn't invite him straight out?'

'No. I'm sure she wants to talk to you first. Does Damon—um—pose a problem, Kent?'

'No, not at all. I didn't mean to give that impression.' He spoke almost too smoothly. 'Bella's right. He's just an old school friend, and it'll be great to catch up with him. Actually, I'd like his email address if that's OK. I presume Bella's already made contact with him?'

Kent sounded relaxed enough, but as they said good-night and Zoe hung up she couldn't help wondering. And worrying.

She wished she'd left it to Bella to tell him about this Damon guy. A bridesmaid was supposed to be tactful and diplomatic. Instead, she'd opened her big mouth and she had the awful feeling she'd stirred up unnecessary trouble.

CHAPTER FOUR

GRABBING a beer from the fridge, Kent snapped the top off, then went out to the back veranda.

The night was hot and still and silent. Low clouds hid the moon and the stars, and the air was heavy and stifling, as if a thunderstorm was brewing.

Tipping back his head, he downed the icy liquid, hoping to wash away the sense of foreboding that hunkered inside him.

Foreboding wasn't an emotion Kent Rigby enjoyed, and it wasn't something that normally troubled him. Most times he was too busy working hard or playing hard. Besides, he liked to keep his life on an even keel and he left the rocking of boats to others. Like Damon Cavello.

Hell.

Kent downed another icy slug, and leaned his shoulder against a timber post, staring out into the black, fathomless night. Talk about lousy timing. Why the blue blazes had Cavello come back now, just when he and Bella had everything sorted and settled?

They hadn't heard from him in years.

Sure, they'd seen his news reports on television, delivered on battlefields while he was dodging explosions and bullets, or emerging from the rubble of an earth-quake, covered in dust and grime.

Damon had made no personal contact with either of them for years. And now Kent and Bella had planned a future together, and they were doing it for all the right reasons.

Everything was working out so well. Tom Shaw was out of hospital and if he continued to follow his doctor's instructions, he'd be OK. He was looking forward to the wedding and walking his daughter down the aisle.

The rosy future Kent had planned was falling into place.

But now this Cavello bombshell had exploded.

Why now?

Zoe sat for ages after she hung up the phone. Curled in an armchair, she almost fell into her old habit of nib-bling at her thumbnail. Actually, she did chew on the corner before she remembered that she had to keep her nails pristine for the wedding. So she chewed on the inside of her lip instead. And pondered.

The vibes for this wedding weren't as upbeat as she would have liked. There were so many undercurrents, not just her own silly crush on the groom—which she *so* hoped no one had guessed—but now, with the arrival of Damon on the scene, there were Bella's and Kent's subtle but unmistakable tensions.

Zoe wished they could all snap out of it. She wanted everything to be rosy and wonderful on planet Bella-and-Kent.

Guiltily, she felt an urge to run away for a bit, but, apart from the fact that she was needed at Willara next weekend, she didn't really have anywhere to go. It was a pity her parents didn't live closer. She would have loved to see her little brother, Toby—to go and watch him play soccer on Saturday afternoon perhaps, or to go surfing with her dad, help her mum make her habitual Friday night curry.

She wondered if Toby knew how lucky he was to live in a cosy house with parents who stayed in one place with a steady job now their dad ran a music store.

One thing was certain. If she ever found the right man, she definitely wanted to settle down and to stay in one place. She wanted her children to go to school with friends they'd known since kindergarten, and she wanted them to play sports together, to make memories together...

Just as Bella and Kent had, and as their children would, too...

Zoe sighed as jealousy coiled unpleasantly inside her. Immediately she felt ashamed of herself. It wasn't as if poor Bella enjoyed a perfect family life. She'd lost her mother. She had no brothers or sisters, and her only family consisted of her ill and grieving father, and a grandparent in an old people's home.

Was it any wonder Bella had turned to gorgeous, steady Kent Rigby and his happy, well-balanced family?

Zoe launched to her feet before she had a chance to feel the lurch of pain that followed any thoughts about Kent. Tonight she was more determined than ever to get over that nonsense. This wedding would be fantastic and she would be the best possible bridesmaid.

Her job for this weekend and over the next few weeks was clear. She had to steer Bella through any muddy waters that surfaced—including old flames—until she arrived safely beside Kent at the altar.

Yes, Zoe felt better now that plan was reaffirmed.

But as she reached for the kettle she saw her hand. Damn! She'd chewed her thumbnail to a nub.

Stripped to the waist, Kent was bending under an outside water tap, cleaning up the worst of the day's grime, when he heard the squeaky hinges of the backyard gate. He looked up, blinked water from his eyes, and saw Zoe Weston poised uncertainly just inside the gate.

She was dressed in city clothes, as if she'd come straight from the office, and her crisp white blouse and charcoal pencil skirt looked totally out of place against a backdrop of gumtrees and grazing land. Kent, however, found himself helplessly captivated.

Stunned might be a better word. He couldn't stop staring.

Zoe's office clothes emphasised her neat, slim curves, and her legs, in sheer stockings and shiny high heels, were—there was only one word—*sensational*. Her dark hair was pulled back beneath a narrow velvet band into some kind of knot, and she looked sophisticated and serious and—heaven help him—astonishingly sexy.

His reaction was as bad as last time. No, worse.

When he'd met her by the road side she'd been wearing a T-shirt and blue jeans. Ever since then he'd worked hard to stop thinking about her unique qualities—not just her sensible calm manner, but the cute tilt of her head, and the blue of her eyes, and the softness of her mouth.

Now, there was something else—something about the sight of her in her smart city clothes that grabbed him by the throat and sent a jolt arrowing south.

Hell.

Why was she here? Alone?

Where was Bella? Weren't Zoe and Bella supposed to be staying at Blue Gums this weekend with Tom Shaw? Tom was so much better now and he'd started going into Toowoomba to the AA meetings.

What had happened?

Shaking off his unwanted reaction, Kent called to her, 'Hello there.'

Zoe still hadn't moved. In fact, she seemed to be as transfixed as he was—watching him with a worried, staring gaze and with a hand pressed to the open V of her snowy-white blouse.

Hastily, Kent snapped off the water and reached for his discarded shirt, using it to dry his bare shoulders and chest as he hurried over to her.

'I wasn't expecting you,' he said, stating the obvious as he thrust his arms into the sleeves of the damp and crumpled shirt. 'Is everything OK?'

'I—' Zoe began, gulping and looking uncomfortable. 'Bella asked me to come here. We were supposed to stay at her father's place, but he's—' She grimaced, and looked embarrassed.

'Oh, no. Tom isn't drunk, is he?'

Zoe nodded. 'He's in a pretty bad way, I'm afraid.'

Kent swore and slammed a balled fist against his thigh. 'Tom was doing so well. He seemed to be on the mend.' He let out a heavy sigh. 'I'm sure Bella's upset.'

'Yes. She begged me to come over to your place, while she stayed with her dad.' Zoe's eyes were round with worry. 'I hope she's OK.'

'She won't come to any harm. Tom's never violent, and he'll certainly never hurt his daughter. Not physically.' Kent pulled the limp fronts of his shirt together, and started to fumble with the lower buttons. 'Just the same, I'll phone her straight away.'

Zoe glanced at his chest and then looked away, her colour deepening.

'Come inside,' he said, doing up another button, then nodding towards the house. 'You look like you could use a cuppa, or maybe something stronger.'

'Thanks. I'd love a cuppa.'

As they walked across the lawn to the screen door at the back of the house Kent's thoughts were for Bella and her devastation over Tom's lapse. He forced himself to ignore the slim, sophisticated woman walking beside him. He paid her no attention. He couldn't afford to think about her curve-hugging skirt and her long legs sheathed in filmy stockings, or her high city heels sinking into the grass.

Sitting at the granite island bench in the Rigbys' farmhouse kitchen, Zoe wrapped her hands around a mug of hot, sweet tea, closed her eyes and drew a deep breath.

From outside came the creamy vanilla scent of wisteria mixed with the danker scent of hay and a faint whiff of animals. But the pleasant country aromas did little to calm her. She was still shaken by the scene she'd witnessed at Blue Gums.

The sight of Bella's father, staggering and incoherent, had been beyond awful, and poor Bella had been so embarrassed and upset. She'd shooed Zoe out of there as quickly as she could.

But Zoe's arrival at Willara Downs had brought an equally disturbing close encounter with Kent's naked, *wet* torso.

OK, a man without his shirt should *not* have been a big deal. Zoe had seen plenty of bare male chests. Of course she had, but this was the first time she'd had a close encounter with Kent Rigby's smooth, bulky muscles, and tapering, hard-packed abs. Not to mention the enticing trail of dark hair heading downwards beneath his belt buckle.

It was an experience destined to rattle any girl senseless. What hope had Zoe?

For pity's sake, she'd gone into mourning over the closure of his shirt buttons…

In fact, Kent had been doing up his buttons crookedly and she'd *almost* offered to help him get them straight. How sad was that? Thank heavens she'd stopped herself just in time.

Now she cringed as she imagined the surprise and disapproval in his eyes if she'd actually reached out and touched him.

It's OK. I didn't do anything stupid. I'm calming down. I'm fine. I'm back in control.

Zoe took another sip of tea and then a bite of the scrumptious shortbread that Kent's mother had thoughtfully left in his pantry. Yes, she was definitely feeling calmer now. And sanity certainly returned as she heard the deep rumble of Kent's voice down the hall. He was talking to Bella on the telephone, and she could imagine him making sure Bella was OK and that her dad was fine, too. He would be reassuring Bella and telling her he loved her.

While their conversation continued, Zoe flicked through a country life magazine with articles about kitchen gardens and new breeds of chickens, and fabulous recipes using all kinds of cheese.

Zoe tried to imagine Bella reading one of these country magazines, and being inspired by the articles. Somehow, she couldn't quite picture her friend getting her beautifully manicured hands dirty in a veggie garden, or rolling pastry, or saving her kitchen scraps to feed to the chooks.

Bella had never actually talked about her future as a farmer's wife. In fact she seemed very much a city girl these days with a fondness for beauty salons and coffee shops rather than hay bales and farmhouse cooking. But then Bella was a bit of a dark horse. She'd never talked about her father's problems with alcohol either.

Clearly there were many strands to Bella's life, and the city office girl who loved high fashion and fancy nail polish was quite possibly a brave front. Now, more than ever, Zoe could understand why her friend had chosen a steadfast and reliable partner like Kent. A good, rock-solid husband. A loving man who knew all about her, a guy who would help to shoulder her worries about her father.

There was no doubt about it. Kent was Bella's perfect match in every way.

Right. OK.

Fortunately, Zoe locked in that thought scant seconds before she heard Kent's footsteps returning down the passage to the kitchen. She had her smile fixed in place before he entered.

Even so, she felt a zap of reaction the instant she saw him. There was something impossibly appealing about Kent Rigby, something about his tanned profile, about his dark, friendly eyes and the flash of his smile that made Zoe feel as bright and shimmering as a sunrise.

Which proved how very foolish she was. Apart from the very important fact that the man was taken—by her best friend, no less—she should have enough bad memories of Rodney the Rat to douse any sparks of unwanted libido.

'How's Bella?' she asked Kent.

'She's upset, of course, and mad as hell with her dad. He'd started going to AA and we thought he was going to be fine now.'

'Perhaps he's just had one slip and he'll be back on the wagon tomorrow.'

'Let's hope so.' Kent let out a sigh. 'Tom had problems with grog when he was young, but he was dry the whole time he and Mary were married. Since her death, he's been on a downhill slide.'

'Poor man. And poor Bella. She must feel so helpless.'

Kent nodded. 'It must have been a shock for you, too, coming across him like that.'

'Well, yes, it was, but only because it was so unexpected. And Bella was so upset.' Zoe lifted her now empty mug. 'Thanks for the tea. It was just what I needed.' She stood. 'I guess you'll want to get over to Bella's place straight away.'

'Later. Tom's asleep right now and Bella wants a bit of time to sort the place out.' Kent went to the fridge, opened it and stood staring at its contents. 'I'll fix a meal for us first.'

'For us?'

'Yep—we're on our own tonight.'

'B-but you don't have to feed me.' Zoe was stammering, rattled by the possibility of a meal alone with this man. 'I can go into town. I'll stay at the pub and grab a meal there.'

'Zoe, relax.' Shutting the fridge once more, Kent grinned at her. 'You're president and secretary of our wedding planning committee. Of course, you're very welcome here. You can stay the night, and you can have the same room as last time.'

She was about to protest again, when she realised it

might come across as rude. Kent was keeping up his reputation for country hospitality. He might be upset if she refused.

'Thanks,' she said. Then, to cover any giveaway signs of attraction, she surveyed the kitchen with her most businesslike glance. 'So what can I do to help you?'

'If we dig out the sheets now, you can make up your bed while I throw a couple of steaks in a pan.'

Already Kent was heading out of the kitchen and Zoe hurried after him. The linen cupboard was in a hallway, and he flipped the louvred doors open, releasing a faint scent of lavender.

'This is where I run into trouble.' A small smile made attractive creases around his dark eyes. 'I haven't a clue which sheets I'm supposed to give you.'

Zoe gulped. Discussing bed sheets with Kent was her wickedest fantasy rolled into her worst nightmare. 'I think I used those pink striped sheets last time.'

'Terrific.' He was already lifting them from the shelf. 'I'm sure they'll do.'

His wrists brushed against her as he handed her the sheets. It was a relief to disappear into the guest room and get busy making the bed.

Once this was done, she freshened up in the bathroom, brushed her hair and changed into shorts and a T-shirt. If only she could switch off her hormones as easily as she changed her clothes.

The scent of frying steak and onions greeted her when she came back into the kitchen. And the rather fetching sight of Kent standing at the stove, changed into a clean white, correctly buttoned shirt.

He sent her another of his flashing smiles, but then

his smile went super still, and he continued to stare at Zoe, a slight frown now warring with his grin.

'What's wrong?'

'You've let your hair down.'

Zap! A bushfire scorched her skin. She fingered her hair, dark and straight like her mum's, and now skimming her shoulders. 'I didn't know it was a crime for a girl to let her hair down on a Friday evening.'

'Course it isn't.' Kent shrugged and turned back to the steaks, flipping them over. Without looking at her, he said, 'It looks great either way. In your bridesmaid's outfit you're going to knock the local yokels for six.'

The comment warranted another very stern lecture to herself. His compliment would go to her head. It should be possible to have a normal conversation with him without overreacting to every second sentence.

Desperate to appear cool and unaffected, she said glibly, 'That's reassuring to know. I'm on the lookout for a spare farmer.'

'Are you?'

It wasn't the flippant or teasing response she'd expected from Kent. His head had jerked around and his dark eyes were surprisingly intense.

Now she was more flustered than ever. 'Of course I'm not serious,' she said tightly. 'That was my poor attempt at a joke.'

Time to put an end to this subject. She looked around her. 'What can I do to help? Why don't I make a salad to go with the steak?'

Kent's thoughts were apparently elsewhere and he took a moment to answer her.

'Sure,' he said at last, and then, after a beat, his usual

smile was back in place. 'Trust a girl to want to spoil a good steak with rabbit food.'

They ate on the back veranda, looking out at the idyllic view of the soft, velvety hills and fields as they were slowly enveloped by the shadowy night.

Zoe wondered what she and Kent would talk about now. Given her recent gaffes, she wasn't sure she could cope with a conversation about Bella and the wedding. She wanted to ask Kent about the property. That was safe, and she was genuinely curious about the crops and grazing herds. Details of farm life had always fascinated her.

But it seemed Kent had other ideas. As he speared a tomato cube and a chunk of cucumber he said, 'So, tell me about yourself, Zoe.'

'Me?'

'Why not?' His smile was relaxed and easy once more and when she hesitated, he said, 'You're Bella's best friend and your friendship's not going to come to an end when we're married. I expect you'll be an important part of our lives for a very long time.'

Would she? Zoe had been hoping that her life beyond the wedding would be Kent-free. How else could she get back to normal? How could she stand the strain of an ongoing friendship with Bella and Kent if they remained close friends way into the future? Good grief, surely she wouldn't still be a jangling wreck when she was eighty?

It was an alarming prospect. Added to that, Zoe didn't really enjoy talking about herself. As a child she'd been forever arriving at new schools and answering the same old questions over and over. 'I've already told you about my parents and how I spent most of my childhood on the road.'

'But your parents have stopped touring now, haven't they?'

She nodded, then took a sip of the chilled white wine Kent had poured for her. And as she put the glass down she found herself telling him about the music shop in Sugar Bay and her little brother, Toby. And then, because he smiled so encouragingly, she told him about Toby's soccer ambitions and his endless experiments and their family's Saturday night barbecues when her parents had jam sessions with old mates.

'Sounds like they're a lot of fun,' Kent said sincerely. 'Would you like to live at the bay?'

'I—I'm not sure.' Zoe pulled a face. 'If I'm honest I feel a bit resentful that Mum and Dad waited till Toby came along before they settled down. He's having a very different childhood from mine.'

She shrugged. 'The bay's a great place to visit, but I like Brisbane, too.' *And the country.* But she wouldn't tell Kent that. 'I have to make my own life, don't I?'

'Of course.' He was watching her carefully again. 'And the world's your oyster,' he said quietly.

'Well, yes… Actually, I'm thinking about heading overseas.'

'You'll love it,' he said, but now his smile was tinged with a bewildering hint of sadness and for the first time Zoe wondered if he felt trapped at Willara Downs.

Curiosity prompted her to say, 'I've often wondered what it's like to grow up in one place and know you'll spend your whole life there.'

'Do you think it sounds boring?'

'No, not at all. Quite the opposite, actually.'

A frown furrowed Kent's brow and his dark eyes registered something very close to dismay.

Fearing she'd said too much, Zoe took a quick sip of her wine.

But whatever had bothered Kent passed and he was soon relaxed again. 'I love living here,' he said. 'It's not just the land and the lifestyle. For me, it's the strong feeling of continuity. My family's been here from the start. My great-great-great-grandfather looked after the horses on one of the earliest explorations and he fell in love with this district and settled here more than a hundred and fifty years ago.'

'Wow.' Zoe looked out at the view that had almost disappeared. 'All that history.'

Kent nodded. 'My grandfather and my great-grandfather both went away to the wars, and while they were gone the women and children ran the farms for them.' Across the table Kent's eyes met Zoe's. 'The responsibility of continuing those traditions means a great deal to me.'

'I'm sure it does. I feel goose bumps just thinking about it.' Zoe loved the idea of such permanence and such a deeply rooted sense of belonging.

'But that doesn't mean I don't love travelling as well,' Kent added with a twinkling smile.

'Have you travelled very far?'

'When I was nineteen I had a year off—backpacking with Steve, my best man, around Europe.'

'What was your favourite place?'

'Prague,' he answered without hesitation.

'That's interesting. Most people choose Paris or London or Rome. Even Barcelona.'

'Or Venice.'

'Yes.' She smiled, pleased that Kent was relaxed

again. When he looked at her with his serious expression, the world seemed to tilt ever so slightly, but everything felt in the right balance again now. 'So what did you love about Prague?'

Kent laughed. 'If Steve was here, he'd rave about the Czech beer. But for me it was the old city at Christmas time. It was snowing and unbelievably beautiful—the buildings, the pavements, the cafés, the restaurants. Everything in Prague is so old and dripping with history. Not a plastic Christmas tree in sight.'

'That sounds lovely. I must remember to try to be in Prague at Christmas.'

'Yes, do that.' For a moment there was a flicker of something in Kent's eyes. It might have been regret, but then he cracked a grin. 'And send me a postcard.'

'I will. I promise.'

'By the way,' he said, 'you still haven't told me your favourite colour.'

'And you haven't told me why you want to know.'

'Patience, Zoe. All in good time.'

'What if said I don't have a favourite?'

He laughed. 'I'd believe you. Neither do I.'

They laughed together then, and for a heady few seconds their gazes reached across the table and locked. For Zoe, it was like the moment beside the road when her entire being had felt connected to Kent's.

Then Kent broke the spell by looking away and deliberately reaching for his beer. And Zoe thudded back to earth. To reality.

She was such an idiot.

After that, they both turned their attention to their meals, but, although Zoe's steak was tender and the salad crisp, she seemed to have lost her appetite. She took another sip of wine and vowed to keep her thoughts firmly fixed on the painful truth.

How could she be so hopeless, when poor Bella was stuck at Blue Gums, caring for her dad? It was Bella who should be here, alone with Kent, and having this nice romantic dinner.

Zoe felt a little better when she and Kent left the veranda and returned to the kitchen to rinse their cutlery and plates and stack them in the dishwasher.

'I hope Mr Shaw will be OK in the morning,' she said.

'Don't worry about Tom.' Kent gave an offhand shrug. 'I'm sure he'll be fine in the morning. He'll be full of remorse and Bella will give him an earful about following doctor's orders.'

Zoe nodded. 'There was a fellow in Lead the Way with a drinking problem. He wanted everyone to turn a blind eye.'

Kent's eyes widened with interest, then abruptly he let out a sigh. 'Got to admit, it's really hard to watch Tom sink into such a state. He used to be such a fine man. He was my hero for many years. He saved my life when I was a nipper.'

'Really?' Zoe couldn't resist asking, 'What happened?'

'I was acting the fool down at the local waterhole, dived in at the wrong spot and hit my head on a rock.' With a sheepish smile Kent leaned closer and pointed to a faint thin scar on his forehead.

Zoe caught the clean, male scent of his skin, mere inches from her. She could see the scar, but his proximity also gave her the chance for a close-up study of the rest of his face, the length of his eyelashes, the graininess of his jaw, the sexy curve of his lips.

Oh, man.

Perhaps Kent sensed her indecent interest. His expression took on a strange frowning tension, and the air around them seemed to pulse. It seemed like ages before he pulled back, and he let out a strangled laugh. 'Lucky I didn't break my flaming neck. I certainly would have drowned if Tom hadn't been there. He got me off the bottom, dragged me out and revived me.'

'Thank God he did.' Oh, heavens, that sounded far too fervent. Quickly, Zoe asked, 'Was Bella there, too?'

'Yes, she witnessed the whole thing. We've both looked on her dad as a hero ever since.'

Kent's voice was so rough and solemn as he said this that Zoe knew deep emotions were tied to the statement.

'I'm sure he'll get over this road bump,' she said gently.

She was also sure it was time for Kent to leave. Regrettably, their time together had been way too pleasant.

She made a shooing motion towards the door. 'Now, thanks for a lovely dinner, but you should get going over to Bella's.'

'Yes, I'll head off now. You know where the tea and coffee are, don't you? And the TV remote.'

'Yes, thanks. I'll be fine. Don't worry about me. I'm used to living on my own. Now, go, Kent. Get out of here.'

He went.

I'm used to living on my own...

Standing at the kitchen window, Zoe watched the twin red eyes of Kent's tail lights disappearing into the black night, and she discovered a huge difference between being alone and being consumed by horrible loneliness.

Dismayed, she went through to the lovely lounge room. Like the rest of the house it was elegant yet relaxing, with deep comfy sofas, brightly coloured throw pillows. With a feminine touch, there'd be cut-glass vases filled with flowers from the garden.

For a brief, unwise moment, she indulged a childhood fantasy and imagined being the mistress of a beautiful country homestead like this one—cutting and arranging flowers from her garden, baking hearty meals for her drop-dead gorgeous, farmer husband and their children, attending meetings of the local growers' association, waking each morning to fresh air and open spaces...

And waking to the drop-dead gorgeous, farmer husband in bed beside her.

OK. Fantasy over. Back to reality. Fast.

Zoe flicked on the TV, made herself comfortable, and settled to watch one of her favourite comedies. A good dose of on-screen hilarity would soon cure her of any lingering self-pity.

But unfortunately the usually lively script was dull and unfunny this evening, and Zoe couldn't raise a chuckle. Her thoughts kept drifting...

She was picturing Kent's arrival at Blue Gums...and Bella's happy, open-arm welcome.

Stop it. Stop it. Stop it.

The couple on the TV screen were embracing, and again Zoe thought about Kent and Bella. Right about now, Bella would probably be undoing the buttons on Kent's shirt, running her hands over his lovely, hard muscles...

Oh, good grief. Enough!

Snapping off the TV, Zoe jumped to her feet. She was *not* going to succumb to this nonsense. She needed to keep busy, to keep her mind occupied with something constructive. But what could she do in a stranger's house?

Heading for the kitchen, she prayed for an answer.

CHAPTER FIVE

KENT was in a black mood. His experience at Blue Gums this evening had been depressing to say the least. Disturbing, too, as he hadn't been able to offer Bella much comfort. She'd been distracted, not her usual self and troubled by more than her father's illness. And yet she wouldn't confide in Kent, wouldn't let him help.

After the pleasant dinner conversation he'd enjoyed with Zoe, his fiancée's reception had been like a bucket of icy water. He was sure it had been a relief for both of them when he left early.

Now, home again, he approached the kitchen and saw...

Candles.

Everywhere.

On every bench top and flat surface in the state-of-the-art kitchen his mother had so faithfully designed, small candles sat, glowing warmly. And in the middle of the dancing candlelight stood Zoe, looking lovely, yet wide-eyed and cautious, rather like a naughty angel caught playing with the devil.

'I'm going to shift all this,' she announced hurriedly as soon as she saw him. 'I was planning to tidy everything before you got back.'

Black mood gone, Kent suppressed a smile as he stepped through the doorway into his kitchen.

'I—I know I've been a little carried away,' she hastened to add. 'I wanted to see how these candles looked, but I wasn't expecting you so soon, Kent. You're early, aren't you?'

'Bella's...worn out,' he said quietly.

'Oh.' Zoe frowned. 'Well, I know you weren't expecting to come home to forty-eight candles, but they're for the wedding. What do you think?'

'They're beautiful.' He gave in to the smile tugging at his mouth. *And you're beautiful, too...*

The thought sprang unbidden, and the words trembled on his lips, but thank goodness he resisted the impulse to voice them aloud.

'I wanted to get the full impact,' Zoe was explaining earnestly. 'I thought the candles would be lovely for the wedding reception. I'd like to put them in little paper bags filled with sand and they should look lovely outside in the garden. But don't worry—they're battery powered, so they're not going to burn your house down.'

'That's a relief.' Stepping closer, Kent lifted a little candle. 'And they can't blow out either.'

'No. They're called smart candles.'

'Good name.' He smiled at her, and he couldn't help adding, 'Smart candles for a smart girl.' Too late, he realised how softly he'd spoken, almost seductively, as if a weird kind of spell had taken hold of him.

In response, Zoe's blue eyes grew wider, clearly surprised. Her lips parted in a small moue.

Kent found himself staring at her soft pink lips... gazing into her lovely, expressive blue eyes...until he was lost in those eyes...

He was in free fall...

And all he could think was how badly he wanted to kiss Zoe. Now. In the middle of his kitchen. Surrounded by the glow of her candles.

He would start by sweeping her into his arms and kissing her sweet, pouty lips, and then he would sample the pale, fine skin at the base of her throat.

But perhaps Zoe could read his mind. She dropped her gaze and a deep stain spread over her cheeks. Her hand shook as she pressed it to her forehead, pushing back a strand of hair with a small sound of dismay.

Kent blinked. What the hell had come over him? Why couldn't he shake off this strange feeling of enchantment?

Zoe was the bridesmaid, for crying out loud. He had to forget about kissing her. *Say something about the candles.*

With a supreme effort, he dragged his attention away from her. What had she said? Something about putting these candles in little bags of sand?

'Do you have the sand you need?' he asked.

Zoe shook her head. 'I—I'm really mad with myself. I meant to call in at a craft shop and I forgot.'

'A craft shop? For sand?'

'In Brisbane the craft shops sell lovely, fine white sand.'

At that, he couldn't help laughing.

'What's so funny?'

'You don't need to buy sand at a craft shop, Zoe. Willara Creek is full of it.'

She shook her head, clearly unimpressed. 'But creek sand is damp and dirty and full of little twiggy bits.'

'Not all creek sand. Why don't I take you down there tomorrow and you can see what you think?' When she hesitated, he said, 'If it's not up to scratch, no harm done.'

'Bella and your mother are both coming over tomorrow. We're going to be busy with all the preparations.'

'We'll go first thing in the morning, then. If you don't mind an early start. How about a quick trip down to the creek before breakfast?'

There was more than a slight hesitation this time, but then Zoe nodded. 'Thank you,' she said, although she didn't smile. Instead she became businesslike. 'I'll shift everything out of here now.' Already she was turning off the candles.

Sitting in bed, Zoe stared into the darkness, unable to sleep.

Hugging her knees, she rocked slightly, something she only did when she was worried.

Or puzzled.

And confused.

The foreboding she'd felt about this wedding was deepening. Something *really* wasn't right—and she was pretty sure it wasn't just her feelings about the bridegroom getting in the way.

She knew Bella wasn't happy and the unhappiness wasn't only related to her father's health problems. Now Zoe was beginning to suspect that Kent wasn't happy either.

This possibility shocked her.

How could such a gorgeous, successful man, who could no doubt have his pick of any girl in the district, allow himself to walk, with his eyes wide open, into a marriage that wasn't gloriously happy?

It was the kind of question that would keep a conscientious bridesmaid awake all night. Pity she'd agreed to be up at the crack of dawn.

When Zoe woke to Kent's knock the next morning she felt more like a sleep deprived bridesmaid than a conscientious one. The thought of leaving her nice comfy bed to look at sand in a creek bed held no appeal.

But Kent had brought her a mug of tea and a slice of hot toast with strawberry jam, and Zoe couldn't help being impressed by this, so she soon found herself in his ute, bumping down a rough dirt track to Willara Creek.

To discover the creek was stunningly beautiful.

Majestic twisted and knotted paperbarks and tall river gums stood guard above water that was quiet and still and cool, and edged by boulders entwined with grevillea roots. Wind whispered gently in the she-oaks.

Charmed, Zoe watched a flight of wild ducks take off from the water. 'It's so beautiful and peaceful,' she said in an awed whisper.

Kent smiled at her. 'I thought you might like it.'

As she climbed out of the ute she heard birds calling to each other as they hunted for honey in the bright red grevillea flowers.

'And here's the sand,' she said, almost straight away seeing a small beach of nice white quartz-like grains.

'There's even better sand over here.' Kent was pointing farther along the bank.

Sure enough, he was right. Trapped among rocks, the sand was so white it glistened. Kneeling, Zoe studied it more closely and saw flickers of gold—pale golden specks, shining brightly. 'Kent, that can't be real gold?'

'No, I'm afraid it's only fool's gold. Its technical name is pyrite. But it's pretty enough for what you want, isn't it?'

'It's perfect. Absolutely gorgeous for a wedding.'

With impressive efficiency, Kent filled a couple of good-sized buckets and stowed them in the back of his ute.

Zoe took a deep breath of the fresh morning air as she looked about her at the deep pool of cool, inviting water, the smooth boulders and magnificent trees. 'I guess we'll have to go back already, but what a pity. It's so beautiful here. It almost looks as if it's been land-scaped.'

'We don't have to rush away.' Kent left the ute and squatted on the bank, looking out across the still water. 'This place has always been special. We've always kept the cattle out of here and we pump water up to troughs for them.'

'It must be amazing to have a place like this that you actually own. You'd feel a very close affinity to it.'

To Zoe's surprise, Kent didn't respond straight away. Picking up a handful of polished river stones, he skipped them out over the water, watching them bounce. As the last stone plopped he said, without looking at her, 'This is where I nearly ended my young life.'

Oh, God.

A pang of horror arrowed through Zoe, and she had a sudden picture of a little boy with dark hair and dark eyes recklessly diving and hitting his head…

This lovely man had nearly died.

Here. In this idyllic setting.

Her throat stung and she might have cried, if Kent hadn't been watching.

He sent her a grin.

She blinked away the tears. 'So this is where Bella's dad saved you?'

He nodded. 'It was nearly a year before I got back in the water.'

'I'm not surprised.' And then, she *had* to ask, 'What was it like, Kent? Can you remember? Did you know you'd nearly died?'

As soon as the questions were out she felt embarrassed by her nosiness, but Kent, to her relief, didn't seem to mind.

'I have no recollection at all of diving in, but I have a very vivid memory of opening my eyes from a deep and terrible, dark dream where I was choking. I looked straight up into Tom Shaw's face, and beyond him I could see the vivid blue sky and the tops of the river gums.'

'Did you know what had happened?'

Kent nodded slowly. 'It's weird, but I seemed to understand that I'd been given a second chance at life.'

He'd only been six—so young to be confronted with something so profound.

'I'm surprised you're still happy to come down here,' she said.

'I love it here,' Kent replied quietly. 'This place always makes me think about survival. And fate.'

'And Tom Shaw.'

His dark eyes studied Zoe's face intently, and again she felt an unwilling connection, a silent *something* zinging between them. Quicksilver shivers turned her arms to goose bumps.

'And Tom Shaw,' Kent said quietly. 'I'll never forget that debt.'

* * *

Shortly after they got back to the homestead, Bella rang.

'How are things at your place this morning?' Kent asked her.

'Dad's fine, thank heavens. He slept in late, but he's just eaten a huge recovery breakfast. And he seems really well. No coughing or shortness of breath. And of course, he's full of remorse and promises.'

'Good. So you'll be coming over here soon?'

'Actually...' An awkward note crept into Bella's voice. 'That's what I'm ringing about. I've been thinking I really should scoot into town to see Paddy.'

'Your grandfather?' Surprise buzzed a low warning inside Kent. 'But Zoe's here. Don't you two have all kinds of jobs lined up for this weekend?'

'Well...yes...but I thought I could squeeze in a *very* quick trip to town. It's just that I haven't seen Paddy for ages and you know how dreary it can be in the old people's home.' Almost as an afterthought, Bella asked, 'Is Zoe at a loose end?'

Kent glanced through the open doorway across the veranda to the garden. His mother had driven out from town to discuss wedding plans and she and Zoe were deep in conversation. They were pacing out sections of lawn and, judging by their arm-waving movements and general nodding and jotting-down of notes, they were discussing the table and seating arrangements.

They'd started over coffee this morning, chatting about the bridal shower—something about making a wedding dress from wrapping paper. Then they'd moved on to the flowers for table centrepieces at the wedding, and the kinds of pot plants that looked best in the gazebo. Zoe had wondered if there should be little lights entwined with the greenery.

The two of them were getting on like a bushfire.

But Kent knew damn well that it should be Bella who was out there in the garden with his mother. Surely, the bride should be involved in all this planning.

Renewed uneasiness stirred in him. He did his best to suppress it. Bella had always been upfront with him. She would tell him if there was a problem.

'Zoe's certainly not at a loose end,' he told her now. 'She and my mother are pretty busy, actually. If you're not careful they'll have the whole wedding planned before you get here.'

'Wonderful,' Bella said with a laugh.

'Wonderful?' Kent tried not to sound too concerned, but he couldn't shake off the troubling sense that something was definitely off kilter. Last night when he'd gone over to the Shaws' place, Bella had been moody and despondent, but that was excusable. He'd understood how upset she was about Tom.

But this morning was different. Tom was on the mend again, and Bella seemed to be leaving all the arrangements for the wedding to Zoe. Surely she should be here?

'You know me, Kent,' Bella said smoothly. 'I've never been much of a planner. Remember how I always used to leave my assignments until the last minute.'

'Yeah, I remember. But I think *you* should remember that Zoe *is* a planner, and hosting a wedding with dozens of guests is hardly the same as a school assignment. Zoe's your only bridesmaid, for heaven's sake, and she's doing an incredible job, but you can't leave it all on her shoulders.'

'Kent, you're right. I'm sorry.' Bella's lowered voice was suddenly contrite. 'I mustn't leave everything to Zoe just because she's so capable. Look, I promise to be out there very, very soon. I'll just race into town, say a quick hello to Paddy, and I'll come straight over. I'll bring a cherry pie and some of that lovely stuffed bread from the Willara bakery for lunch.'

Still worried, Kent hung up and stood with his hand resting on the receiver. He frowned as he looked through the doorway to his mother and Zoe out in the garden.

They were examining a bed of roses now, heads together—one a shower of silver curls and the other a silky, dark brown fall. The two of them were talking animatedly and doing rather a lot of smiling and nodding.

Zoe leaned forward to smell a lush pink rose bloom, and her hair swung forward with the movement. She was wearing knee-length khaki shorts and sandals, and a soft floral top with a little frill that skimmed her collarbones—so different from yesterday afternoon's pencil-slim skirt, stockings and high heels, and yet every bit as appealing.

The women moved on, and his mother became busy with her secateurs, tidying, trimming, and apparently explaining something to Zoe. Every so often, a tinkle of feminine laughter floated over the lawn.

Watching them, Kent thought that any stranger, coming upon the idyllic scene, could be forgiven for assuming that Zoe was his mother's future daughter-in-law.

His bride.

Hell. A dangerous flame leapt in his chest. Hell no. Not Zoe. It was ridiculous. Impossible. Never going to happen.

Bella should be here. Now.

* * *

As it turned out, Zoe also made a trip into Willara that morning. Having settled on their plans for the bridal shower, she and Kent's mother needed several items from the newsagent, so Zoe volunteered to collect them.

'Perhaps Kent could go with you for company,' Stephanie Rigby suggested.

Out of the corner of her eye, Zoe saw Kent tense, and felt an answering whip-crack reaction. *No.* No way could she risk spending any more time alone with her best friend's bridegroom.

Without chancing another glance in Kent's direction, she said, 'Thanks, but I know Kent's busy, and I'll be fine on my own.'

To her relief, there was no argument.

'You never know your luck,' Stephanie said serenely. 'You might run into Bella and you could double check her preferences before you buy the ribbons and the paper daisies.'

'That's a good idea. I'll keep an eye out for her. I guess Willara's so small, it's quite possible to run into people on the main street.'

Stephanie laughed. 'It happens all the time.'

'Your best chance of catching Bella will be at the Greenacres home or the bakery,' Kent suggested in a dry, unreadable tone that made Zoe wonder if he was in a bad mood.

'OK, I'll try the home, then the bakery.'

Zoe had never visited a home for the aged. Her grandparents were still quite fit and healthy and lived in their own homes, so she was already a bit nervous when she pulled up at Greenacres on Willara's outskirts. Then she walked through sliding doors into the large, tiled foyer, and came to a frozen, heart-thudding halt.

Bella was standing on the far side of the reception

area, deep in conversation—an animated, intense conversation—with a young man.

Zoe took one at Bella's companion and immediately recognised the wild, dark hair and strong stubbled jaw from the photos she'd seen on the internet. Damon Cavello.

She felt a punch of shock in the centre of her chest, but she told herself she was overreacting. Damon was an old friend of Bella's and Kent's from their school days— and a chance meeting with him in an aged care home was perfectly harmless. It wasn't as if she'd caught Bella indulging in a sly assignation. This was no big deal.

So maybe they were leaning subtly towards each other and gazing intently into each other's eyes. And maybe their body language suggested a deep, mutual interest that locked out the rest of the world…

Or maybe Zoe was totally misreading the whole situation.

Unable to contain her curiosity a moment longer, she stepped forward. 'Bella!'

Her friend jumped and turned, and when she saw Zoe she blushed like litmus paper.

'Zoe, f-fancy seeing you here.' Bella shot a hasty glance to the man at her side, then back to her friend. 'Are you looking for me? Nothing's happened at home, has it?'

'There's no problem,' Zoe reassured her. 'I came into town to buy a few things from the newsagent, and I ducked in here first. We knew you were here and we'd like to have your approval on—'

Zoe hesitated, uncomfortably aware of Damon Cavello's steely and not particularly friendly gaze. 'We wanted to check on one or two—matters—for the wedding.'

'Oh, right.' Bella was her normal colour again, and she straightened her shoulders and lifted her chin, drawing dignity around her like armour. She smiled carefully as she turned to the man beside her. 'Damon, this is my bridesmaid, my wonderful friend, Zoe Weston.'

Despite the tension zinging in the air, Zoe was aware of a warm swelling of pride when she heard herself described in such glowing terms.

'Zoe, this is Damon Cavello, an old school friend.'

'Of course.' Zoe held out her hand and favoured him with her warmest smile. 'You contacted me on Facebook. Hi, Damon, nice to meet you.'

'How do you do, Zoe?' Damon shook her hand firmly, but his smile didn't quite reach his eyes. 'And thank you for engineering this chance to hook up with the old gang.'

He nodded towards Bella and his silver-grey eyes seemed to smoulder, but his voice was relaxed enough, so it shouldn't have been an awkward moment. Zoe, however, could feel unmistakable vibes of tension. And yikes, she could practically see the electricity sparking between this pair.

'Damon has been visiting his grandmother,' Bella said.

'And you ran into him while you were visiting your grandfather. What a lucky coincidence.'

'Yes.'

An elderly woman, shuffling past with a walking frame, beamed a radiant smile on the three of them.

'Well...as I said, I was on the way to the newsagents,' Zoe continued. 'So if you two have more catching up to do, I can wait for you there, Bella.'

'It's OK. I'll come with you now. Damon and I have said our hellos.'

Damon frowned and Zoe sent him another friendly smile. 'Will we see you at the wedding?'

'Sure.' He swallowed uncomfortably as if there was a painful constriction in his throat. 'Kent kindly emailed an invitation. Asked me to the bucks' party as well.'

'Great. We should run into you again, then, either some time next weekend, or on the big day.'

'Absolutely.'

The girls had driven into town in separate vehicles, so there was no chance for an in-depth conversation during their shopping jaunt or on their separate journeys back to Willara Downs. And for the rest of the weekend they were so busy, making decorations, or party favours, or cooking sweets and canapés to be stored or frozen that they didn't have time for an in-depth talk.

It was Sunday afternoon when they were heading back down the highway to Brisbane before they were alone and the subject of Damon could be properly aired.

Not that Bella was in a talkative mood. From the moment they left Willara, she seemed to slip lower and lower in the passenger seat, slumped in despondent silence.

'Missing Kent already?' Zoe asked tentatively.

Bella gave a guilty start and she frowned like a sleeper waking from a dream. 'Sorry...what did you say?'

'I asked if you were already missing Kent.'

'Oh...yes...of course.'

'At least you'll only have to wait two more weeks and then you can be with him all the time.'

'Yes,' Bella said softly.

Zoe had used every ounce of her inner strength to remain upbeat and supportive about Bella's good fortune, despite all the worrying niggles. Surely her friend could try a bit harder to act happy. Instead of rallying, however, Bella seemed to sink into even deeper misery.

By now, they were heading down the steep Too-woomba Range, and Zoe couldn't take her eyes off the road, but she had the horrible feeling that Bella was on the verge of crying. Then she heard a definite sob.

Casting a frantic sideways glance, Zoe saw tears streaming down her friend's face. Her heart gave a sickening lurch.

'Bell,' she cried, keeping her gaze fixed on the steep, winding road. 'What's the matter?'

'I'm OK,' Bella sobbed. 'I'm just being an idiot.'

Zoe couldn't help wondering if Damon was somehow the cause of these tears, but she had no idea how to ask such a probing question. Besides, it was her duty to keep Bella focused on Kent.

'It must be awful to have to say goodbye to Kent every weekend.'

'Oh, Zoe, don't,' Bella wailed.

Don't? Don't talk about Kent?

Thoroughly alarmed, Zoe held her tongue as she negotiated a particularly sharp hairpin bend. Out of the corner of her eye, she was aware of Bella pulling tissues from the bag at her feet and wiping her eyes and blowing her nose.

It wasn't till they reached the bottom of the range and the road levelled out once more that Zoe stole another glance Bella's way. Her friend was no longer crying, but her face was pale and blotchy and she still looked exceedingly unhappy.

'I really don't want to pry, Bell, but is there any way I can help?'

Bella released a drawn-out sigh. 'I don't think so, thanks.'

'I mean—tell me to shut up, but if you want to talk—about—*anything*—it's the bridesmaid's job to listen.'

This was greeted by a shaky little laugh. 'Oh, Zoe, you're such a sweetheart.'

A nice compliment, but not exactly true. A sweetheart did not fall for her best friend's fiancé.

A few minutes later, Zoe tried again. 'So…I suppose it's just tension. You have so much on your plate just now—worrying about your dad, and so many jobs crowding in with the wedding so close.'

Bella turned away to look out of the window at rows and rows of bright sunflowers standing with their heads high like soldiers in formation.

Clearly, she wasn't looking for a chance to talk about her problem, so Zoe drove on in silence…wondering… worrying…

Then out of the blue, as they approached Gatton, Bella sat up straighter. 'Zoe, I think I do need to talk. I can't deal with this on my own. Can we pull over?'

CHAPTER SIX

Zoe took the next ramp leading off the highway and parked beneath a jacaranda tree in an almost empty picnic area. At a distant table, a family were gathering up their tea things and packing them into a basket. The mother was calling to her little girl who was scooping up fallen jacaranda blossoms.

Suddenly needing air, Zoe lowered her window and dragged in deep breaths, catching the dank scent of newly turned earth from nearby fields and the sweeter scent of the flowering trees.

Her stomach churned uncomfortably and she unbuckled her seat belt. She was dead-set nervous now that Bella was about to confide her problem. Her friend's tears pointed to a serious dilemma, and Zoe wasn't confident she had the wisdom or the strength to advise her.

Honestly, could she trust herself to put her own silly, unwanted emotions aside?

Praying she would get this right, she said gently, 'I'm ready whenever you are, Bells.'

Bella pulled another tissue from her bag and blew her nose noisily, then, after only a moment's hesitation, she took the leap. 'There's no point in beating about the bush. I'm in a mess about this wedding.'

'Ah-h-h.'

Bella shot Zoe a sharp glance. 'So you're not surprised?'

'Not entirely. I must admit I've been waiting for you and Kent to show more—er—emotion about—well—everything. And right from the first time Damon made contact, it was pretty clear he made you edgy.'

Bella nodded. 'I know. Seeing Damon again has been a kind of wake-up call.'

'You mean you really care about him?'

'Oh, I don't really know, Zoes. He sends me kind of crazy. It's like I'm still in high school. Up and down and all over the place.'

'I'm sorry. I should never have posted that rave about your wedding on Facebook. It's my fault Damon found you.'

'Gosh, don't blame yourself. I think he heard about the wedding from other people as well.' Bella was pulling the tissue in her lap to shreds.

'Damon's not trying to stop you getting married, is he?'

Zoe had a sudden vision of Damon Cavello calling out in the middle of the wedding—at that moment when the minister asked the congregation to speak up or for ever hold their peace.

Bella shook her head, then, with another heavy sigh, she kicked off her shoes and drew her feet up onto the seat, hugging her knees. 'The thing is, when Damon rang me on Saturday morning, I had to see him. I thought if I saw him just once in the flesh—if I spoke to him, I'd get the old memories out of my system. But as soon as we met—'

Hairs stood on the back of Zoe's neck as she watched the flush spread across Bella's face. She tried to make light of it. 'So your heart took off like a racehorse? Your knees gave way?'

Bella nodded, then covered her face with her hands. 'What am I going to do?'

It was a question Zoe didn't want to answer. But poor Bella hadn't a mother to turn to and she was her best friend. Praying for wisdom, Zoe took a deep breath before she spoke. 'I—I guess it all depends on how you feel about Kent.'

At first Bella didn't answer. When she did, her voice was soft, wistful… 'That's my problem. I'm so worried that Kent and I are marrying for all the wrong reasons.'

'But he's stop-and-stare gorgeous,' Zoe suggested miserably.

Bella shot her a sharp, surprised glance.

'Just stating the obvious.' Zoe's shoulders lifted in a defensive shrug, and a dull ache curled around her heart.

'Well, I'm not going to argue with your good taste,' Bella said with a watery smile. 'But I just wish Kent and I had been in some sort of long-term relationship, or had at least been dating. The truth is, we haven't really seen very much of each other since I moved to Brisbane. We only caught up again properly when I started coming home, because Dad was so sick. We were both so worried about Dad and the farm, and Kent's gone out of his way to help.'

And he feels he owes your dad big-time for saving his life, Zoe wanted to say, but she kept the thought to herself.

Instead she said, 'I never totally understood how your engagement came about. It seemed a bit out of the blue to me. What made you say yes in the first place?'

Bella looked down at her diamond engagement ring

and her stunning, dark berry fingernails—enviably dramatic and gorgeous. 'It was a bit of an emotional whirlwind. It's not all that long since I lost my mum, and then it looked like I was losing my dad as well. The farm was going to rack and ruin. I felt like I was going under, too.'

'And yet you never mentioned anything about it to me.'

'Well…to be honest, I was a bit ashamed about my dad's drinking.'

Zoe gave a guilty sigh. If she'd been a better friend, the *right* kind of friend, Bella might have felt more comfortable about sharing her worries.

'I was coming home every weekend,' Bella went on. 'And I started seeing more and more of Kent, and he was so sweet, so supportive. He's been running our property as well as his own. And of course we have a deep bond that goes way back. Then one weekend, he just looked at me and said "Why don't we just do it? Why don't we get married?"'

Bella was smiling at the memory. 'In a flash, it all seemed to make wonderful sense. It was the perfect solution, and you should have seen the smile on Dad's face when we told him. He was *so* relieved I was being taken care of.'

To Zoe it was now blindingly obvious why Bella and Kent were marrying. Kent felt a huge debt to Tom Shaw. Bella was in danger of losing her family, her farm—losing everything, in other words. Bella and Kent had a long history, a shared background that made them suited to each other in every way. Duty and friendship had won, and Kent had saved the day.

Everything might have been fine if Damon hadn't arrived on the scene, no doubt reawakening Bella's school-girl fantasies of passion and romance…

Oh, man… Zoe's thought winged back to Friday night when Kent arrived home to find his kitchen filled with candles. Her skin flamed at the memory of the way he'd looked at her…

The flash of fire in his eyes had shocked her. Thrilled her. As had the roughness of emotion in his voice.

And next morning, there'd been another moment of connection down on the creek bank…

No, she mustn't think about that now. She mustn't let her own longings confuse Bella's situation.

In fact, Zoe knew she mustn't do or say anything to influence Bella right now. She had no similar experience to draw on, no wisdom to offer. Her role was to listen…

But surely Bella must see all the benefits of this marriage? Her life could be fabulous if she went ahead with it. Kent was perfect husband material. Gorgeous looks aside, if you factored in his easy manner, his beautiful home and garden, his prosperous farm and country lifestyle in a friendly, close-knit community, Willara Downs was like the closest thing to heaven.

Then again, Zoe knew that her nomadic childhood had given her a longing for security and a love of being settled that Bella might not share.

And yet, for Bella there was the added advantage that, with Kent as her husband, her father would almost certainly recover and grow stronger. Every day he would see his daughter happily married and living close by. It was such a strong incentive for Tom to throw off his bad habits and take care of his health.

Surely these were weighty plusses.

Bella, however, was sighing. 'I was so emotional at

the time Kent came up with the wedding proposal. But I know he only made the offer because he was worried about Dad, and he felt he owed something to my family. He's always had a highly developed sense of doing the right thing.'

'So he was being heroic instead of romantic?'

'Yes,' Bella admitted in a small voice.

A marriage of convenience. The thought suffocated Zoe.

Again, she forced her own longings aside. She had no doubt that Kent possessed the necessary strength of character to make a success of anything he set his mind to. Even if his marriage wasn't based on passion, he would be a loving and loyal husband.

'But the marriage could still work,' she said softly.

Bella turned to her, her eyes wide with dawning hope. 'That's true, Zoe. Even arranged marriages can work out happily.'

'So I've heard,' Zoe agreed, trying not to sound deeply miserable. Perhaps it was melodramatic of her, but she felt as if she were saying goodbye to her own last chance for happiness.

Bella was looking down at her sparkling engagement ring. 'So...you think I should go ahead and marry Kent?'

An agonising pain burst in Zoe's throat and she swallowed it down. She opened her mouth to speak, but changed her mind, afraid she might say something she'd regret.

Bella sat up straight. 'It *is* the right thing to do,' she said with sudden conviction. 'Kent's no fool. He wouldn't have offered to marry me if he wasn't happy about it.' She shot Zoe a pleading glance. 'Would he?'

Tension made Zoe tremble. She could feel the sharpened claws of her jealousy digging deep, but she forced a shaky smile. 'From where I'm looking, you'll have a wonderful life with Kent.'

She held her breath as Bella sat, staring through the windscreen, her eyes bright and thoughtful. Outside the car, the light was fading. A gust of wind sent jacaranda bells fluttering onto the windscreen.

'But you're the only one who can make the final decision,' Zoe said at last.

'You're right. I shouldn't be putting pressure on you like this.' Nevertheless, a smile dawned on Bella's face, as pretty as a sunrise. She took Zoe's hands and squeezed them tightly. 'I know what I must do. Damon threw me off track. He's always been dangerous like that. But Kent and I made our decision for all the right reasons and we should stick to our original instincts.'

Leaning forward, Bella kissed Zoe's cheek. 'Thank you for helping me to sort this out.'

Tears stung the backs of Zoe's eyes and she blinked madly to hold them back. 'No problem. Point thirty-nine in the bridesmaid's handbook. Lots of brides have second thoughts as the big day approaches.'

'I'm quite normal, then. That's a relief.'

Zoe tried to crack another smile, but couldn't quite manage it.

It didn't matter. Bella's arms were around her, hugging her tight. 'I'm so lucky,' she whispered. 'I have the best bridesmaid in the world.'

CHAPTER SEVEN

To KENT's relief, his bucks' night wasn't too extreme. He'd heard of bridegrooms being tied naked to a pole in the main street, or bundled into a crop-dusting plane and transported to a remote outpost.

Fortunately, his best man, Steve, wangled just the right tempo. He'd done a great job of rounding up Kent's mates and the party was a blast. Not a city-style bash with strippers and pranks—just blokes enjoying themselves in a quiet country pub. Actually, the quiet country pub was growing rowdier by the minute, but the revelry was harmless enough.

There were the usual games with drinking penalties. Right now, anyone who raised taboo topics—cricket or football, the bride or her bridesmaid, the share market or politics—had to down his drink in one go. Merriment by the bucketful.

Later they'd sleep it off in the Mullinjim pub, and there'd be a few sore heads in the morning, but at least there was still a full week before the wedding.

Of course there were all kinds of comments flying about Kent's last chance for freedom.

It was a phrase that made him distinctly uneasy— but he wasn't prepared to dwell on that. He imagined most guys felt the cold snap of an iron noose about their throats whenever they thought too hard about the doors closing behind them when they stepped up to the altar.

One week to go...

He'd be glad when the tension was behind him, when he and Bella were safely settled...

Tonight, however, he had to put up with the good-natured ribbing from his mates, had to laugh as he agreed that his days as a carefree bachelor were numbered. But he wondered what the others would think if they knew how often his thoughts trailed back to earlier this evening when he'd driven through Willara and caught a glimpse of the girls at the pub.

Already in party mode after the bridal shower, Bella's friends had all been there, in shiny strapless dresses in a rainbow of colours. Looking like gaudy beetles, they'd wolf-whistled and waved glasses of pink champagne at Kent as he drove past.

He hadn't seen Bella, but she would have been in the mob somewhere, no doubt sporting a mock bridal headdress concocted from a piece of mosquito netting and a plastic tiara.

The girl he *had* seen and noted was Zoe.

She'd been standing in a doorway, chatting with a friend, and she was wearing a dress of striking tangerine silk, an exotic colour that highlighted her dark hair and slim elegance.

For a split second as Kent flashed past her eyes had met his. Startled, she'd half raised her glass.

He'd only caught that fleeting glimpse of her in the bright dress with one shoulder bared, but the image had shot a scorching flame through him. He'd remembered her in his kitchen, surrounded by four dozen smart candles and he'd felt that same thrust of longing he'd felt then.

Now, Kent consoled himself that this was the dop-
pelgänger that haunted most men about to be married—
the alter ego taking a final backward glance at freedom
before diving into monogamy.

Get over it, man.

But even now, as he chatted and joked with his mates,
his brain flashed to the memory.

Of Zoe. Not Bella.

Damn it, if he'd seen Bella at the pub he wouldn't be
plagued by these memories now. He'd be thinking only
of Bella, not Zoe with her shiny dark hair and soft smile.
But now, instead of focusing on his bride, a treacherous
part of his brain kept pressing rewind, kept replaying
a picture of Zoe's slender curves encased in a sunburst
of silk.

Why the hell now? Why tonight?

'Kent, old mate. Need to have a word.'

The voice behind Kent brought him swinging round.

Damon Cavello, glass in hand—a double shot of neat
whisky by the look of it—greeted him with a morose
smile.

They'd talked earlier, fighting to be heard above the
hubbub, but it had been a superficial catch-up, skimming over the past decade in half a dozen carefully ed-
ited sentences. Now Damon held out his hand.

'I've overlooked congratulating the lucky bridegroom.'

'I'm sure you said something earlier.' Kent accepted
the handshake uneasily, wondering if he'd detected a
hint of stiffness in Damon's manner.

'You know you're a very lucky man,' Damon said.

'I do indeed.'

'You deserve her, of course.'

'Thank you.'

Why did he have the feeling that Bella's old flame was testing him? Rattling his antlers, so to speak.

Damon offered a mirthless grin. 'Bella's a—'

'Hold it!' Kent laughed as he raised his hand. 'There's a penalty tonight if you mention the bride's name.'

'Damn, I forgot.'

Before Kent could let him off the hook, Damon tossed down the contents of his glass.

Kent inhaled sharply, imagining the fire lacing the other man's veins.

'So, where was I?' Damon asked as he set the empty glass on the bar. 'Ah, yes.' Folding his arms across his chest, he sized Kent up with a knowing smile. 'I was agreeing that you've made an excellent choice of bride. You and your future wife will be the toast of Willara.'

Kent accepted this with a faint nod.

Damon's gaze shifted to a point in the distance beyond Kent's shoulder. His chest rose and fell as he drew in a deep breath, then exhaled slowly.

To Kent's dismay, the other man's eyes betrayed a terrible pain. 'I was a fool,' he said, his voice quiet yet rough with self loathing. 'I was the world's biggest fool to head off overseas, leaving her behind.'

A nightmare weight pressed down on Kent, crushing the air from his lungs and stilling his blood. He pulled himself together. 'That may be true, mate,' he said slowly. 'You were famous for doing crazy things back then. You were legend.'

'I was, but I regret it now.'

What was Damon implying? Was this some kind of mind-game strategy?

'Are you trying to tell me something?' Kent challenged in a deliberately exaggerated country drawl. 'Are you saying that you would have married young and settled down with a mob of kids in quiet old Willara?'

'Who knows? We can't turn back time.' Damon squared his shoulders, looked about him at the happy crowd, then whipped back to Kent. 'Promise me one thing.'

Kent eyed the other man levelly, refusing to be intimidated. 'What's that?'

Temporarily, Damon lost momentum. Dropping his gaze, he tapped a short drumbeat on the smooth timber-topped bar. When he looked up again, his grey eyes were blazing ice. 'Just make sure you don't have any doubts, my friend, not the slightest shadow.'

The words struck hammer blows, but Kent refused to flinch. 'Thanks for your advice,' he said coolly. 'It's heartening to know there's another man in town who understands how lucky I am to be marrying Bella Shaw.'

Looking Damon in the eye, Kent downed his drink.

It was well past midnight when Zoe heard the tap on her door. She hadn't been asleep, although her body was worn out from the huge effort of running both the bridal shower and then the hen night. The functions had been proclaimed a great success, but now her brain couldn't stop buzzing.

When the soft knock sounded, she slipped quickly from the bed, went to the door and opened it a crack. Bella was outside in the dark passageway, wild eyed and wrapped in a pink-and-blue kimono.

'Can I come in for a sec?' she whispered.

'Sure.' Zoe readily opened the door, but threads of fear were coiling in her chest. All night she'd been watching Bella with mounting alarm.

While the bride had laughed and chatted and joined in the silly, light-hearted party games, Zoe had been aware of the underlying pulse, a ticking time bomb of tension. Plainly, things still weren't right for Bella. The strain showed in her eyes, in her smile.

Luckily, all the other party girls had been too busy drinking and having a good time to notice. But Zoe, who'd taken her hen night responsibilities seriously, had mostly drunk tonic water.

Clear-headed, she'd noticed plenty and she'd worried plenty. Most especially, she'd worried that Bella still wasn't happy with the decision she'd reached last week.

Now, her friend collapsed into the only chair in the room. 'I've just had a text from Kent,' she said. 'He wants to see me. To talk.'

'Tonight?'

'Yes, but I said it was too late. I rang back and talked him into leaving it till first thing in the morning.'

'Do you know what he wants to talk about?'

'He wants to make sure I'm totally happy about—' Bella let out a soft groan. 'He wants to discuss the wedding.'

Zoe's heart thudded. 'I assume this isn't just a planning meeting.'

'No. I'm pretty sure he wants to double check that we're both still on the same page.'

'About getting married?'

Closing her eyes, Bella nodded.

'What are you going to tell him?'

A sob broke from Bella. 'I have to be totally honest, Zoe. I don't think I can do it.'

CHAPTER EIGHT

For ages after Bella went back to her room, Zoe tossed and turned, her sheets damp with sweat, her thoughts rioting. Eventually, she got up and shut the window and switched on the air conditioning, but, although the system was efficient and the room cooled quickly, she couldn't settle down.

Everything was spinning round and round in her head. Bella's distress, Kent's ultimatum, the mystery surrounding Damon—and, of course, the beautiful wedding reception she'd planned....

Time crawled. It took for ever for dawn to finally arrive as a creamy glow around the edges of the curtains. Giving up any pretence of sleep, Zoe rolled out of bed and opened the curtains to a view down Willara's main street. At this early hour the little town was empty and silent, and it looked a little faded, too, like a ghost town in an old black-and-white movie.

Was Kent already on his way?

She showered and shampooed her hair, then blow-dried it and packed her bags, shoving all the leftover party glitter, shredded cellophane, cardboard and felt pens into an outside pocket. She had no idea why she was saving this stuff, couldn't imagine ever using it again.

There'd been no special arrangements made for breakfast—all the hen-night girls wanted to sleep off the party after-effects. But Zoe's room had started to feel like a jail cell. She knew Bella wouldn't eat until after she'd spoken to Kent, so she decided to go downstairs to dine alone.

As she went past Bella's door she thought she heard the soft murmur of voices. Perhaps, even now, Bella and Kent were making a decision. Just thinking about it made Zoe's eyes and throat sting with hot tears.

The hotel's dining room was old-fashioned with dark panelled walls and vases of bright flowers on the tables. It was still very early, and the room was empty, but a girl was there, ready to take orders.

Zoe glanced at the menu. It offered a full country breakfast with bacon, scrambled eggs, mushrooms and fried tomatoes, but, while she'd been ravenous an hour ago, her anxious stomach rebelled now.

She ordered tea and toast and sat in a sunny corner near a window. She was drinking her second cup of tea and eating hot buttered toast spread with local orange marmalade when a tall, broad-shouldered figure appeared at the dining-room doorway.

Kent.

Zoe's knife clattered to her plate.

Had he already spoken to Bella? If he hadn't, what was she supposed to say?

Kent came across the room, weaving past the empty tables covered by clean white cloths. He sent her a cautious smile, but it was impossible to gauge his mood.

He didn't look utterly heartbroken, but perhaps he was very good at masking his feelings. He was definitely paler than usual and there were shadows under his eyes, as if his night had been as restless and as tormented hers.

'I was hoping I'd find you,' he said when he reached her.

'Have you seen Bella?'

'Yes. We've been talking in her room for the past hour.'

A chill skittered over Zoe's arms. She was still unsure how to handle this.

'Can I join you?' Kent asked.

Zoe nodded, and once he was seated she realised she'd been holding her breath. The tension was unbearable. What had they decided?

Kent placed his hands squarely on the table. 'I wanted you to be the first to know. Bella and I are calling off the wedding.'

Zoe's heart gave a painful thud. Even though this wasn't totally unexpected, she felt as if she'd stepped from solid ground into thin air. 'I'm so sorry.' Tears stung her eyes and her throat. 'I can't begin to imagine how you must be feeling right now, Kent.'

'It had to be done,' he said with a shaky smile.

Zoe didn't know how to respond to that. She was dazed—and shell-shocked.

No wedding.

After all the excitement and planning and busyness of the past few weeks—now, nothing. *Nada.*

'How's Bella?'

'She's worn out from over-thinking this whole deal, but she's OK, I guess, or at least she will be after a good night's sleep.'

'I should go upstairs to see her. She might want some friendly support.'

'Actually, she's not here.' Kent lifted his hands in a

don't-ask-me gesture. 'She had to rush off to Green-acres. There's been some sort of problem there.'

'No…not her grandfather?'

'I think so.'

'Oh, God. Poor Bella. As if she hasn't had enough to worry about.'

'I offered to go with her, but she said she wanted to handle it herself, which was understandable, I guess.'

'Maybe there's something I can do?' Zoe was already rising from her chair.

'I told Bella to ring if we can help.'

As Zoe sat once more she let out a sigh. Her mind flashed to her excitement when Bella first asked her to be a bridesmaid. Who would have thought it would come to this?

The waitress appeared at Kent's side. 'Would you like to order breakfast, sir?'

'Ah, no…but perhaps some tea. Zoe, shall we order a fresh pot?'

Considering the awkwardness of their situation, Zoe found his politeness and self-control impressive. As soon as the girl had left she reached across the table and squeezed Kent's hand. It was meant to be a comforting gesture, but for her the brief contact still sparked the usual silly electricity.

'Thanks for being such a good friend to Bella,' he said.

Zoe gave a rueful shake of her head. 'My big chance to be a bridesmaid. Gone down the tube.'

'You would have been perfect,' he said warmly.

'Well, for that matter, I thought you and Bella would have been the perfect couple.'

'Did you really?'

Tension shadowed his lovely dark eyes as he waited for her answer.

Zoe found herself suddenly flustered. 'You had so much in common.'

'Maybe that was the problem.'

The waitress returned with the tea and a fresh cup and saucer for Kent, so they became busy with pouring and helping themselves to milk and sugar.

When they were alone again, Kent said, 'Zoe, the decision to call the wedding off was mutual.'

She was almost giddy with relief. 'Gosh, I'm—I'm—'

'Mad with us both for messing you around?'

'No, I'm not mad. If I'm honest, Kent, I've been worried for ages. The vibes weren't right between you.'

Kent grimaced and rubbed at his jaw in a way that was intensely masculine.

'But for what it's worth,' Zoe added, 'I think your motives for proposing were honourable.'

'What do you know about my motives?'

'I don't want to say anything out of place, but I'm guessing you wanted to look after Bella, and you wanted to put Tom's mind at ease.'

Kent's mouth tilted in a lopsided smile. 'You're not just a pretty bridesmaid, are you?'

Despite everything, Zoe drank in the sight of him sitting opposite her in his moleskin trousers threaded with a crocodile leather belt.

'The truth is,' he said, after a bit, 'I had a revealing chat with Damon last night. We started off toe to toe like two duelling bucks, all bluster and bravado. But then I started really listening to the guy. He was talking about Bella, and I watched his face, his body language. I heard the depth of emotion in his voice...'

Kent paused and his impressive chest expanded as he drew a deep breath. 'I don't know if he's the right man for Bella, or if she even wants him, but last night I found myself questioning—everything. I realised that I was denying Bella—denying both of us the chance to have a marriage based on something *more* than friendship.'

He was looking directly at Zoe and she felt heat spreading over her skin. She told herself to stop it. Just because Kent was no longer marrying Bella, she couldn't start imagining he was going to dive into a new relationship. And even if he did, why would he choose her?

Suddenly, with her role as bridesmaid swept away, her old insecurities were rushing back.

She was relieved when Kent returned to practicalities.

'I've told Bella I'll take the heat as far as the wedding's concerned. I'll talk to our families and friends.'

What a task. Zoe pictured the girls upstairs. They'd be getting up soon and would have to be told the news, and there were so many others who would need to know. It was all going to be awkward and embarrassing, and Kent was shouldering the load. She felt a rush of sympathy for him, another layer to add to the emotional storm inside her.

'Perhaps I could help with ringing the caterers and the hire people?'

Kent considered this. 'I'd like to say don't worry. You've done more than enough, and I'll take care of it. But with all these other calls to make, I'd really appreciate your help, Zoe. As it is, I think I'll be spending all day on the phone.'

On cue, Kent's mobile phone rang and he quickly retrieved it from his pocket. 'It's Bella,' he said as he checked the caller ID.

Zoe watched the concern in his eyes as he listened. She tried not to eavesdrop, but she couldn't help catching his rather alarming responses.

'Do you think that's wise, Bella?... What about the police?... Yes, I've spoken to Zoe. I'm with her now. Yes, sure.'

To Zoe's surprise, he handed her the phone. 'Bella wants to speak to you.'

'What's happening?' she whispered.

He rolled his eyes. 'Big drama. Bella will explain.'

Heavens, what else could go wrong? Zoe lifted the phone. 'Hi, Bella.'

'Zoe, I'm so sorry I dashed off, but you won't believe what's happened. My grandfather and Damon's grandmother have taken off.'

'Taken off?' Zoe almost shrieked. 'You mean they've run away from Greenacres? Together?'

'Yes. They've taken Damon's grandmother's car.' Bella's sudden laugh was almost hysterical. 'It's ridiculous, I know. It might only be a prank, and they're not senile or anything, but we can't let them drive off together without knowing what they plan to do. We have a lead, so Damon and I are going after them.'

'Far out. That's—that's incredible.'

'I know. I can't believe it either. But, Zoe, I'm really, really sorry to be abandoning you. I wanted to talk to you this morning, to explain everything.'

'Don't worry about me.' Lowering her voice, she said, 'Kent's explained about the wedding.'

'Is he OK?'

Zoe sent a glance Kent's way. Catching her eye, he gave her another crooked smile and she felt a flash of useless longing. 'He seems to be bearing up.'

'Zoe, can you look after Kent? Keep an eye on him?'

'I—I—' Zoe was so thrown by the thought of ongoing contact with Kent that she wasn't quite sure what to say. And yet, she couldn't overlook the pleading in Bella's voice. 'Yes, yes, of course I will.'

'Thank you. Thanks for everything, Zoes. I'm so sorry you're not going to be my bridesmaid after all, but at least we can be thankful we chose a dress you can wear to a nice party.'

Zoe rolled her eyes. The last thing on her mind was her dress.

'I'll stay in touch,' Bella said. 'But I've got to dash now. Talk soon. Bye.'

'Bye. And, Bella—'

'Yes?'

'Be careful, won't you?'

'Um…yeah, thanks for the warning.' Bella spoke softly, as if she knew very well that the warning was mostly about Damon Cavello.

Dazed, Zoe handed the phone back to Kent. 'I'm beginning to think I must be dreaming. Runaway grandparents, for crying out loud! None of this is happening, is it?' She held out her arm. 'If someone pinched me now, I'm sure I'd wake up.'

Laughing, Kent took her arm, and his warm fingers encircled her, creating a bracelet of heat. Instead of pinching her, however, he stroked a feather-light caress on the fine, pale skin of her inner wrist.

A tremor vibrated through her, and she gasped. Had he felt it?

His dark eyes flashed a message—inchoate and thrilling—unmistakable.

Her heart thundered. *Don't be an idiot.*

He was still watching her as he released her. He smiled. 'I'm quite sure you're wide awake.'

Then, as if to correct himself, he became business-like once more. 'Now,' he said. 'It's time to get cracking. We have a wedding to cancel.'

Rusty hinges squeaked as Kent pushed open the old timber gate that led to the tangle of shrubbery and weeds surrounding the Shaw family's homestead. Even on a pleasant spring afternoon, the unkempt jungle looked depressing—a far cry from the beautiful, prize-winning garden that had been Bella's mother's pride and joy. Mary Shaw would roll in her grave if she could see this mess now.

Kent called out, partly in greeting, partly as a warning. 'Tom, are you home?'

Tom's faithful border collie appeared, eyes eager and bright and tail wagging happily. Mounting the front steps, Kent greeted him. 'Where's your boss, Skip?'

'I'm in here,' called a deep male voice. 'In the kitchen.'

Relieved, Kent made his way down the hall, but his gut clenched as he thought of the task ahead of him.

He'd already broken the news about the wedding to his parents and they'd coped surprisingly well. His mother had made a gentle complaint about all the money she'd spent on her outfit.

'Where am I going to wear a brocade two-piece in Willara?' she'd demanded, with a rueful smile, but she hadn't really looked unhappy.

His father had given his shoulder a sympathetic thump and muttered that he was proud of Kent's courage.

And Bella had spoken to Tom, of course, so Kent wasn't about to drop a bombshell.

Just the same, as he entered the big, airy kitchen at the back of the old timber Queenslander it was hard to shake off the feeling that he'd let Tom Shaw down.

Kent looked about the kitchen filled with windows and painted sunshiny yellow. It had always been his favourite room in this homestead. In his primary school days, he'd regularly dropped in here for afternoon tea.

There'd always be home-made macadamia or ginger cookies and milk, and he and Bella had eaten them at the scrubbed pine table, or sometimes they'd taken their snack outside to sit in their cubbyhouse beneath an old weeping willow.

Now, Kent found Bella's father standing at the greasy stove, thin, unshaven and pale, with heavy shadows under his eyes. At least he appeared to be sober, which was something, and he was stirring the contents of a pot with a wooden spoon.

This Tom Shaw was such a different figure from the man Kent had known and admired for most of his life. It had been a rude shock to watch this man slide downhill so quickly and completely after his wife's death. He'd hated to stand by and witness his hero's self-destruction.

So, yeah…the wedding plan had been all about propping Tom up again. Now, Kent squared his shoulders.

'Evening,' Tom greeted him morosely.

'Evening, Tom.' Kent stood with two hands resting on the back of a kitchen chair, bracing himself.

'Bella rang and she explained about the wedding.'

'Yeah.' Kent swallowed. 'I'm sorry it hasn't worked out.'

'Well…actually—' Tom smiled wryly '—I'm relieved, son.'

'Relieved?'

Tom nodded. 'I know I was excited at first. It's true I was thrilled with the notion of you taking care of my Bella and Blue Gums. I could die happy. But it wasn't long before I realised something was missing. Something really important.'

Turning the flame down beneath his cooking pot, Tom folded his arms and leaned back against a cupboard. 'I've been in love, Kent. I had a great marriage, full of spark.' He fixed Kent with knowing eyes. 'That's the thing. There has to be a spark—something beyond friendship. Something to set your soul on fire.'

Kent knew he was right. This lack of a spark was exactly what he and Bella had finally acknowledged. They were very fond of each other. They were great mates. But deep down they knew the passion they both yearned for was never going to materialise.

'I'm ashamed that you were both prepared to take that huge step for my sake,' Tom said. 'Heck, Kent, marriage is a gigantic step.' His eyes took on a little of their old fire. 'I couldn't bear to think you were tying the knot to repay me for yanking you out of the flaming creek all those years ago.'

'But I owe you my life.'

'I happened to be on the spot, and I just did what anyone would have done.' Tom shook his head. 'Thank heavens you and Bella have come to your senses.'

Kent took a moment to digest this. He had a sneaking suspicion that his parents were as relieved as Tom was, although they hadn't expressed their views quite so strongly.

'I'm glad you understand,' he said quietly. 'But while we're being honest, there's something else I need to get off my chest.'

'What's that?' The other man's eyes narrowed.

Kent's grip on the chair tightened. 'It's your turn to wake up, Tom. I know it's been hard for you these past eighteen months, but you need to accept that no one else can take responsibility for your health. I can plough your fields and mend your fences, and I can even offer to marry your daughter, but none of that will help you if you can't give up your bad habits.'

Tom dropped his gaze, jaw stubbornly jutted. 'You're dead right. In fact, I'm one step ahead of you.'

'Have you rejoined AA?'

'I have and I won't miss another meeting. That last time I put on a turn in front of Bella's friend was my wake-up call. I really let Bella down.'

Kent gripped Tom's hand. 'That's great news, mate. Well done.' Now he was grinning widely. 'Doc King gave you plenty more years if you conquered the grog and worked on your fitness.'

'Yeah, so that's the plan. I want to be around to see my grandkids.' Tom gave Kent's shoulder a hearty bang. 'And your nippers, too.'

At the end of the day Zoe stood on the back veranda at Willara Downs, looking out at what had fast become her all-time-favourite view. She'd had a huge weekend and was almost dead on her feet, and Kent had insisted that she couldn't possibly drive back to Brisbane this evening.

So while he'd gone to talk to Tom Shaw, she'd prepared dinner—lamb baked with garlic and rosemary and lemon.

For an afternoon, she'd been living her fantasy—fussing about in a farmhouse kitchen, cooking a tasty dinner for the handsome farmer who belonged there.

Which only proved how foolish she was. It was time to put this episode behind her, time to forget about Kent.

The emotional connection she felt towards him and his beautiful home was out of all proportion to her true relationship. She was nothing more than Kent's former fiancée's *almost* bridesmaid.

OK. So maybe she'd promised Bella she would 'look after' Kent, but surely the kindest thing she could do was to leave quickly and without any fuss. Later she would stay in touch via email. Emails were safe.

Even though she knew all this…for now, she was enjoying her last look at this lovely view. Beyond the fence bordering the homestead's lawns and gardens stretched fields of sun-drenched golden corn and green pastures dotted with grazing cattle. Beyond that again, distant low hills nestled in a purple haze.

For Zoe there was something magical about it, especially now when it was tinged by the bronzed-copper glow of the late afternoon.

When she was small, she used to look out of the window of her parents' bus at views like this. At this time of day she would see farmers on their tractors, turning away from the chocolate earth of their newly ploughed fields and heading for home.

As the bus trundled down the highway she would watch the lights coming on in farmhouses, spilling yellow into the purple shadowed gardens. She'd watch wisps of smoke curling from chimneys into skies streaked with pink and gold and lavender. Sometimes she caught glimpses through windows of families gathered around kitchen tables.

Most evenings, shortly after dusk, her parents would turn in at a camping ground. Zoe and her mum would need a torch to find their way to the shower block, and they'd hurry back, damp and sometimes shivering in their dressing gowns. Her parents would cook a meal on their portable gas stove, and Zoe would do her homework, or read a book, or listen to the radio.

The bus was cosy enough at night, but oh, she'd coveted those warm, sturdy farmhouses. For Zoe, the simple ripple-iron-roofed dwellings surrounded by crops and fields were more beautiful and desirable than any fairy-tale castles.

Remembering those days now, she leaned on the veranda railing, drinking in details to keep them stored in her memory. The scent of newly cut grass. The deepening shadows creeping over the fields. The soft lowing of cattle. And coming from behind her, the fragrant kitchen aromas.

'I thought I might find you out here.'

Zoe turned, deliberately slowly, and smiled as Kent came to rest his arms on the timber railing beside her.

'Now everyone who needs to know knows,' he said. 'I had to leave messages for one or two folk, but at least they've all been informed.'

'How did Tom take the news?'

'Surprisingly well.'

'Wow. You must be relieved.'

'Very.' He turned, folded his arms and regarded her with a quizzical smile. 'Dinner smells good.'

'Yes, you have impeccable timing. The roast is due out of the oven right now.'

Together they went into the kitchen and Kent opened a bottle of wine. It felt incredibly domesticated and intimate to Zoe. But then, she was in full fantasy mode, while Kent was getting over a huge ordeal.

Nevertheless, he looked very much at home, pouring wine, wielding a carving knife, slipping a light jazz CD into the player. And he was lavish with his compliments for Zoe's cooking.

'I had farm-fresh ingredients,' she said. 'How could I go wrong?'

Across the table, Kent sent her a smile. 'Pity you're heading back to Brisbane tomorrow.'

It was silly to feel flustered, but there was a glitter in his dark eyes and a husky rumble in his voice that set Zoe's pulses dancing a crazy jig.

'So what are your plans for the rest of your week off?' he asked.

'Actually, I've been thinking that I might as well go back to work.'

Kent's eyebrows shot high. 'And waste the chance to take a holiday?'

'I'm not in the mood for a holiday now, and I can save this week for later. For when I go overseas.'

'Ah, yes. Christmas in Prague. Is it all planned?'

'No. I need to start booking my flights as soon as I get back.'

Kent frowned and dropped his gaze. A muscle jumped in his jaw.

'What about your plans, Kent? I know you had time set aside for a honeymoon. Are you still going to take a break?'

He shrugged. 'Not much point really. Besides, it's

the dry season and I need to keep the feed supplements up to the cattle. There's more than enough to keep me busy around here.'

Zoe was quite certain he was making excuses, but she understood. Under the circumstances, he wouldn't enjoy a holiday on his own. For her, getting back to work was about keeping busy and stopping her mind from revisiting endless if onlys...

It would be the same for Kent, magnified one hundred times.

Zoe left Willara Downs after breakfast the next morning. For the last time, she stripped the pink-and-white sheets from the bed in the pretty guest bedroom, and looked around fondly at the space she'd foolishly begun to pretend was hers.

Now it was time for reality. Back to the city. She needed to get over her silly crush on Kent, and the only way to achieve that was to stay well away from him.

Her car was parked at the side of the house, behind a hedge of purple-flowering duranta, and Kent insisted on carrying her bags, while she carried the bridesmaid's dress.

After laying it carefully along the back seat, she stepped back and took a deep breath. Time to say goodbye. *No tears, now.*

She offered Kent her best attempt at a smile.

But to her surprise he was staring at the dress, which was now a filmy river of coffee and cream chiffon on the back seat. 'You would have looked so lovely in that,' he said in a strangely choked voice.

Zoe tried to laugh. 'It's ridiculous how badly I wanted to be a bridesmaid.' She shook her head at her own foolishness.

'You've been perfect anyhow, a perfect *almost* bridesmaid.' He flashed a brief quarter-smile. 'Bella couldn't have had better support.'

'Nice of you to say so.' Zoe squeezed the words past the tightness in her throat. 'But if we talk about all that now, I'm going to make a fool of myself.'

Determined not to cry, she opened the driver's door, tossed her shoulder bag onto the passenger's seat, and slipped the key into the ignition. She was blinking madly, trying so hard to be strong.

'Zoe,' Kent said softly, and his hand closed around her arm.

She ducked her head, hoping he couldn't see her struggle.

'Zoe, look at me.'

He spoke with such convincing tenderness she couldn't bear it. She was swiping at her eyes as he turned her around.

'Hey...' With the pads of his thumbs, he dried her tears.

Electrified, she was zapped into stillness by his touch. He was so close now she could see the tiny flecks in his eyes—fine streaks of cinnamon combined with hazelnut—could see his individual eyelashes...

'There's something I need to give you,' he said and he produced from his jeans pocket a slim gold box.

'What is it?'

'Your bridesmaid's gift.'

Shocked, Zoe clapped a hand to her mouth. She shook her head.

'Come on,' he said, smiling as he pushed the box into her free hand. 'You've earned this, and I went to a lot of trouble to get the right colour.'

'Oh.' Her hands were shaking.

'Here, let me open it for you.'

She watched as Kent's big hands lifted the dainty lid to reveal a bracelet made of beautiful, translucent beads of every colour.

'They're made of hand-blown glass designed by a local artist.'

'Kent, they're gorgeous.' Each bead displayed a uniquely different rainbow of colours, but the overall effect was one of beautiful harmony. 'I love it. Thank you so much.'

Setting the box on the bonnet of her car, Kent took her wrist. Oh, the intimacy of his hands, of his warm strong fingers brushing her skin. A wave of longing and regret crashed over Zoe and she was in danger of crying again. She closed her eyes to hold the tears back. Then, to her utter surprise, she felt Kent's hands cradle her face, tilting it ever so slightly towards him.

Her eyes flashed open and for breathless seconds they stared at each other, and she saw surprise—the same surprise she was feeling—mirrored in Kent's eyes.

Surprise and disbelief…

And knowledge…

And helplessness…

And then he was kissing her.

Or Zoe was kissing him.

Or perhaps they simply flowed together, drawn by a potent, irresistible magnetism, as if by some miracle they shared the same aching need, the same unspoken longing.

Zoe's senses revelled in the scent of Kent's skin, and the dark taste of coffee on his lips, the thrilling strength of his arms wrapped around her. She was quite sure she'd never been kissed with such wanting, and she certainly knew she'd never returned a kiss with such fervour.

When they drew apart, at last and with great reluctance, they stood facing each other, panting and flushed and slightly self-conscious.

When Zoe spoke, she tried to sound a thousand times more composed than she felt. 'That was unexpected.'

'For me, too. But I'm not complaining.'

No. Zoe wasn't complaining either, but she felt compelled to offer reasons…excuses… 'It's been an emotional weekend. I—I guess I needed a hug.'

'I guess you did,' Kent agreed with a smile.

'And I—ah—should be going.' She turned back to the car again. Already the magic was fading, and the reality of their situation was rushing back. They'd both been under amazing strain and the kiss was an emotional finale to an incredibly emotional weekend.

Nothing more. Certainly nothing to weave dreams around.

What could she say now? *So long, it's been good to know you?* If she looked at Kent again, she might make a fool of herself, so she spoke without turning back to him. 'I'll let you know if I hear from Bella.'

'Thanks, and I'll pass on any news from my end.'

'Emails are probably the easiest.'

'Sure.'

Deep breath. 'Goodbye, Kent.'

'Bye.'

He took a step closer, and dropped another warm kiss on her cheek. Zoe's insides were doing cartwheels. 'See you later. Maybe,' she choked.

'Make that definitely,' Kent corrected quietly.

She didn't reply and closed the car door. He tapped

on her window with his knuckle, and they waved to each other.

Her eyes welled with tears, but she blinked them clear. *Enough of this nonsense.* They'd finished this story. This was…

The End.

She took off, watching Kent in her rear vision mirror. He stood with his feet firmly planted, his hands sunk in his pockets…watching her…and when she reached the end of the drive and was at last enveloped by the tunnel of trees, he still hadn't moved.

CHAPTER NINE

To: Zoe Weston<zoe.weston@flowermail.com>
From: Kent Rigby<willaraKR@hismail.com>
Subject: The Runaways
Hi Zoe,
I hope you had a safe trip back and that everything was fine when you got home. Just wanted to thank you once again. I don't think you truly realise how big a help you've been.

Also, I've had a text from Bella, and she and Damon are still on the trail of the grandparents. They're heading north—staying in Rockhampton tonight, I think.

Are you determined to go back to the office tomorrow?

Seems a shame you can't have a decent break.
Cheers,
Kent

To: Kent Rigby<willaraKR@hismail.com>
From: Zoe Weston<zoe.weston@flowermail.com>
Subject: The Runaways
Hi Kent,
Thanks for your email and for asking if everything

was OK, but I'm afraid I came home to a minor disaster. I asked my neighbour to take care of my goldfish while I was away and she overfed them, so my poor goldfish, Orange Juice, was floating on the top of a very murky tank. By the looks of it, Anita dumped half a tin of fish food in there.

I didn't think to warn her that you can't do that with goldfish. Thank heavens I wasn't away all week or I would have lost Brian and Ezekiel as well. As it is, they look a bit peaky.

I know you must be thinking I'm a screw loose to be so upset about a goldfish, but they're the only pets I can have in this flat, so they're important. Now, I've spent most of the evening cleaning the tank.

But, yes, to answer your question, I'll be back at the office in the morning.

Bella sent me that text, too. It's a weird situation they've found themselves in, isn't it? We can only hope it all works out happily.

Best wishes and thanks again for your hospitality, Zoe.

To: Kent Rigby<willaraKR@hismail.com>
From: Zoe Weston<zoe.weston@flowermail.com>
Subject: Thank You

Kent, you shouldn't have. Honestly. It was so sweet of you to have a goldfish delivered to the office.

The delivery boy caused quite a stir when he appeared in the doorway with a huge grin on his face and a plastic bag with a goldfish in his hand.

As if the office gossip wasn't already flying thick

and fast this morning. Quite a few of the girls were at the hen party, so of course the whole staff wanted details.

Luckily, when the delivery came I got to the door first, so no one else saw the docket and realised it came from you. That would certainly have put the cat among the goldfish, and everyone would have been jumping to the wrong conclusions.

But I'm very grateful, Kent. According to a magazine article on feng shui, three goldfish in a tank are always better than two, so your gift has restored my chances of inner peace and prosperity.

And I'm sure you'll be pleased to know that the new fish is very pretty, with lovely white markings and delicate fins. I've decided she's a girl and I've called her Ariel.

Brian and Ezekiel are very impressed.

Thank you again, and warmest wishes,

Zoe

P.S. I'm off to book my overseas trip tomorrow—with Christmas in Prague as a must.

To: Zoe Weston<zoe.weston@flowermail.com>
From: Kent Rigby<willaraKR@hismail.com>
Subject: Re: Thank You

I'm so pleased the delivery arrived safely. Sorry that it caused a stir in the office, but at least feng shui has been restored in your household. I hope you enjoy your new fish.

No news from the northern adventurers, but I'm assuming they're still hot on the trail.

Hope the travel bookings go smoothly. I'm jealous.
Cheers
Kent

The confession of jealousy was no lie. As Kent pressed send he could think of nothing he'd like more than to take off for Europe again. With Zoe.

He imagined showing her all the places he'd discovered—taking a ride on the London Eye and drinking a pint in a quaint old English pub. Dining out in Paris, or walking through the Latin Quarter. In Spain they would visit art galleries and sample tapas bars. They'd walk Italy's magical Cinque Terre. Experience Christmas in Prague.

Together.

He'd decided that Zoe would be a perfect travel companion. She was organised and yet easy-going, adaptable and fun. Sexy.

Yeah, if he was honest, he was utterly absorbed with the idea of kissing Zoe in every location. Their farewell kiss replayed in his head on an almost continuous reel.

He tried to tell himself that he was overreacting, riding on a tidal wave of relief now that he was no longer marrying someone out of a sense of friendship and duty.

So, OK, there'd been plenty of sparks. With Zoe he'd experienced the very fireworks that had eluded him and Bella. Serious sparkage that left him hungry for more than mere kisses. But Zoe was back in Brisbane now, and soon she'd be heading overseas. A man with a grain of common sense would look elsewhere.

Problem was, this man had experienced his fill of common sense. Now he wanted nothing more than to indulge in fantasies. And he kept remembering Zoe surrounded by dozens of smart little candles, kept picturing her on the bank of Willara Creek, her face soft with emotion and empathy, wanting to understand. He saw her on the road side struggling with a flat tyre. In the pub on the hens' night, in a sexy dress, bright as a flame. He remembered drying her tears just before he kissed her. Goodbye.

Zoe knew it was silly to keep checking her private emails at work and then to rush to her laptop as soon as she got home. Silly to be disappointed when there was no new message from Kent.

She wanted to move on and to put the entire Willara experience behind her, so Kent's silence was a step in the right direction.

Now that she was home, and had a little distance, she could see how dangerous her penchant for Kent had been. After her painful, harrowing heartbreak over Rodney, she was mad to hanker for another man who'd just called off his engagement.

Even though Kent and Bella's relationship had been very different from Rodney and Naomi's, the patterns were too close for comfort.

Besides, she suspected that Kent wasn't looking to settle down. She'd heard talk at the hens' night that he used to play the field, and, of course, he'd recently pulled out of commitment to Bella. It was true; he'd been gallant to the end. Just the same, he certainly wouldn't be ready to leap into a new, serious relationship.

Once and for all she had to move on. Kent's kiss had been nothing more than a spontaneous outburst of feelings at the end of an extremely emotional weekend.

And his thoughtfulness in sending the goldfish was just another example of his general niceness.

His email silence, on the other hand, simply meant there was no news from Bella—and it was a perfect opportunity for Zoe to move forward.

His silence was a desirable result. Honestly.

Very slowly, over the next twenty-four hours, the straightforward sense of this started to sink in. Zoe focused on planning her holiday.

It was going to be quite different travelling solo instead of travelling with Bella as she'd once hoped. Quite an adventure, really.

On Friday evening when Zoe arrived home from work, she was deliberately *not* thinking about Kent Rigby. She most especially concentrated on *not* thinking about him when she heard a knock on her front door.

Having just kicked off her shoes, she answered the door in stockinged feet—a distinct disadvantage when her caller was six feet two. No doubt that was why she blurted out inhospitably, 'What are you doing here?'

Kent had the grace to look a little embarrassed. 'I had business in the city and I was passing by.'

It might have been the lamest of excuses, but Kent Rigby in the flesh could obliterate Zoe's protests and doubts with a single warm smile.

One glance into the twinkling dark depths of his eyes and all her resolutions to forget him flew out of the window.

'So,' she suggested, trying to subdue her happy grin. 'I suppose you've dropped by to see how Ariel's settling in.'

'Ariel?'

'Your thoughtful gift. My new goldfish.'

Kent laughed—a lovely, sexy masculine rumble. 'Of course. I've had sleepless nights wondering. How is she?'

Zoe stepped back to let him through her doorway, conscious of his height and size and her lack of shoes and the supreme smallness of her living room. The fish tank sat rather conspicuously at one end of the low set of shelves that also held her television set.

With a wave towards it, she said, 'Ariel's the pretty one with the dainty white fins.'

Kent sent a polite nod towards the tank. 'She's a very fine specimen.'

'As you can see, she's quite at home now.'

'She is. That's great.' But he immediately switched his attention from the fish and back to Zoe. 'I know this is a bit last minute. I would have called at the office earlier today, but you were worried about wagging tongues.'

'You could have telephoned.'

'Yes.' His smile tilted. 'But I wanted an excuse to see you.'

Not fair. Zoe's resistance was melting faster than ice cream on a summer's day. Desperate to hang on to her diminishing shreds of common sense, she said, 'I haven't heard from Bella, have you?'

'Yes, she rang this morning.'

'So they're still heading north?'

'Yes, and there's an awful lot of coastline, so heaven knows how long it will take.'

Standing in the middle of her living room, Kent was watching her, unabashedly letting his eyes rove over her work clothes, her legs…

Self-consciously, she fiddled with the bridesmaid bracelet at her wrist. Unwisely, she'd taken to wearing it constantly. She rubbed one stockinged foot against the other.

He smiled again. 'So…how are you now, Zoe?'

'I'm—I'm fine.' What else could she say? She could hardly admit to feeling up and down and all over the place after one goodbye kiss. 'More importantly, how are you?'

'I'm OK. Surprisingly OK, actually.'

Memories of their kiss hovered in the air. Recklessly, Zoe thought how easy it would be to drift towards him again, to find herself in his arms, tasting that lovely, seductive mouth.

She struggled to remember all the reasons it was wrong. *He's free to play the field now. Don't get hurt. Remember Rodney!* She found refuge in her duties as a hostess. 'Would you like to sit down, Kent? Can I get you a drink?'

Instead of answering, he asked, 'Am I interrupting your plans for Friday night?'

'I—I was planning to have a quiet night in.' She'd been looking forward to a stress-free weekend for a change.

'So I can't tempt you to a quiet dinner out?'

Oh.

Zoe's mouth worked like her goldfish's. She'd spent the past week listing all the reasons why she must stop swooning over this man. Rodney the Rat had featured high on that list. Kent's own reputation as Willara's most dedicated bachelor was another point worth remembering. But now—*shame on her*—now that he'd asked, she couldn't think of anything she'd like more than to go out with him.

Besides, she'd promised Bella she'd keep an eye on

Kent—and going out with him tonight was simply doing Bella a favour, wasn't it?

'Dinner would be lovely,' she said, trying to strike the right note between polite and casual. 'Why don't you make yourself at home while I change into something more—?' Zoe bit off the word *comfortable*… It was such a cheesy cliché and she didn't want to give Kent a whiff of the wrong idea.

'Let me get you a drink,' she said instead. Her kitchen led off the living area and she went to the fridge and opened it. Unfortunately, she hadn't been in the mood for shopping this week, so there was half a bottle of rather old white wine, the heel of an ancient block of cheese and a handful of dried apricots.

Thinking of the bounty at Willara Downs, she felt extremely inadequate in the hostess department.

'I don't need anything now. I'm happy to wait till dinner,' Kent said, watching her from the doorway. 'And you don't need to change. If you don't mind coming as you are, I think you look great in that outfit.'

'In this?' Zoe repeated, amazed. She was still in her work clothes—a dark green skirt and a cream blouse with pintucking and neat little pearl buttons.

Kent's eyes twinkled. 'Yes, in that. You have no idea how good city clothes look after a steady diet of jeans and Akubras.'

Given her own love of all things rural, Zoe had quite a fair understanding of how the trappings of a very different world might appeal.

So, five minutes later, having once again donned her high heels and given her hair and make-up a retouch, she was in Kent's ute and heading for her favourite suburban Thai restaurant. Fleetingly, she wondered if she should be wary or on guard, but such caution seemed impossible. She was ridiculously happy.

Apart from the huge fact that she was being escorted by a gorgeous guy who caught every woman's eye, she'd always loved this particular eating place. She loved coming through the swing glass doors to be enveloped by the fragrant and exotic aromas wafting from the kitchen. And she loved the sumptuous yet relaxing ambience—rich pink walls adorned with mirrors in dark, intricately carved wooden frames, and tables covered in cloths of peacock and gold.

She enjoyed the little rituals, too, like the basket of pale pink prawn crisps that came along with their menus. This evening, sharing one of her favourite places with Kent, she was filled with bubbling excitement.

They decided to choose exotic steamed fish, and chilli and ginger paste chicken. Then their drinks arrived—a glass of chilled white wine for Zoe and an icy beer for Kent—and they nibbled the prawn crisps and sipped their drinks. And they talked.

Wow, how they talked.

To Zoe's surprise, Kent did *not* bring Bella or the wedding into their conversation. He started by asking her more about her travel plans, and he told her about the places he'd enjoyed most when he'd been overseas. They moved on to movies and discovered they both loved thrillers. They talked about books, but Kent preferred non-fiction, so there wasn't quite so much common ground there.

They might have moved on to music, but their meals arrived in traditional Thai blue-and-white bowls and they soon became busy with helping themselves to spoonfuls of fluffy jasmine rice. The delicious fish had been baked in coconut milk with slices of ginger, and the chicken had been stir-fried with masses of vegetables.

Everything was wonderfully hot and spicy and at first they were too busy enjoying themselves to talk about anything except the food, but then Kent asked, out of the blue, 'Are you very ambitious, Zoe?'

Ambitious? Thrown by the question, she stared at him. Her most recent goal had been to be a perfect bridesmaid. Apart from that, she wanted to travel, but her biggest ambition was to find the right man, to settle down and start a family, which was the last thing she'd admit to this man.

Fleetingly, she remembered her childish dream to live in a farmhouse that sat safely and squarely in the middle of green-and-gold fields. She hastily dismissed it.

'Actually, I don't think I can be very ambitious,' she said. 'I like my job and I want to be good at it, but I have no desire to smash through glass ceilings.' She pulled a face. 'Don't tell your feminist little sister.'

Kent grinned. 'Your secret's safe with me. Perhaps you're content.'

No. Content she was not, especially since she'd met Kent. Lately, restless yearning had been her constant companion.

She doubted that Kent would want to hear her true ambition—to settle down with the right man, to put down roots, raise a family.

'My parents have never been go-getters,' she told him instead. 'Lead the Way might have been a huge success, if they'd had a bit more tooth and claw.'

'And you might have been the child of celebrity rock stars.'

'Imagine.' Zoe rolled her eyes. 'Actually, I think my

parents would have hated all the celebrity fuss that goes with being famous. I can't imagine my mother being a diva, stamping her foot because the limo wasn't pink.'

She laughed at the impossibility of the picture. 'What about you, Kent? Are you ambitious?'

'I have big visions for the farm—projects like land management and tackling environmental issues. It's easier to try new methods now I'm managing Willara on my own. My dad wasn't keen to change and Tom's just as bad. They want to keep doing things the way they always have. Pair of dinosaurs, both of them.'

There was passion in his voice, which surprised Zoe. 'I must admit every time I was at Willara I was always so caught up with the wedding I didn't give much thought to the business and management of your farm. But it must be quite an enterprise. You're like a CEO of your own private company.'

'Yes, and it keeps me busy.'

'But you love it.'

'I do.'

Kent smiled that special way of his that launched Zoe into outer space. Yikes, she had to calm down. Tonight was all about friendship.

Sure, there were sizzles and sparks that zapped her whenever she looked across the table. And yes, there were dark flashes of appreciation in Kent's eyes. And, most certainly, she was aware of a deepening sense of connection when they talked.

But this wasn't a date. Kent hadn't once tried to flirt with her, or to touch her, or to offer her the over-the-top compliments that Rodney had trotted out on their first date. This evening was humming along at a nice, safe, just-friends level.

Reassured by this success, Zoe found herself asking

recklessly, 'Are there any other ambitions? Do you still plan to marry and have a family one day?'

Kent stiffened with obvious surprise.

Oh, good grief. What an idiot she was.

He concentrated on helping himself to a final spoonful of fish. 'Right now I can't imagine ever lining up for another wedding.'

'And who could blame you?' Zoe said fervently.

To her relief, her awkward question didn't ruin the night. As they left the restaurant and walked into the sensuous magic of the warm spring night the scent of frangipani and honeysuckle hung in the humid air. From a pub down the road a band was sending out a deep pulsing beat.

Kent reached for Zoe's hand, threaded his fingers through hers. 'Thanks for bringing me here. It was a fabulous meal.'

'My pleasure,' she said softly, while her skin tingled and glowed from the contact.

When they reached his car, he opened the passenger door for her, and she was about to get in when he said, 'Wait a minute.'

She turned and he gently touched her cheek. 'I just wanted to tell you—you look lovely tonight.'

Her skin flamed with pleasure. 'Thank—'

Her reply was cut off by his kiss.

Which wasn't exactly a surprise—all night she'd been teased by memories of their other kiss.

This kiss was different and yet utterly perfect. Beyond friendly—oh, heavens, yes—but not pushy. Just slow and sexy and powerful enough to make Zoe hungry for more.

She was floating as she settled into the passenger seat, and it wasn't till they pulled up outside her flat that she came to her senses. It was time for a polite, but hasty exit.

A kiss was one thing, but becoming more deeply involved with this man was way too risky. He might be the most attractive man she'd ever met, but tonight he'd admitted that his long-term goals were the polar opposite of hers. She wanted to settle down. He didn't.

It was all very black and white.

'Thanks for a lovely evening, Kent.' Already, her fingers were reaching for the door handle.

'Zoe, before I forget, I have something for you.' Reaching into the back seat, Kent picked up a brown-paper packet.

'Another gift? But you've given me a bracelet and a goldfish.' She hoped this wasn't going to be chocolates or flowers—the clichéd trappings of seduction.

'It's just a book,' he said. 'I thought it might come in handy.'

She caught the dark gleam of his eyes as he smiled at her through the darkness. A book, a nice safe book. Tilting the packet, she let it slip onto her lap. It was a hardback with a glossy cover. They weren't parked near a streetlight, but there was just enough light for her to make out the title.

'A book about Prague. Gosh, how thoughtful of you.'

Flipping it open, she saw beautiful, full-page co-loured photographs, but the dim light couldn't do them justice. It seemed rude not to invite Kent inside.

'I need to make you coffee before you tackle the long drive back,' she explained in case he got the wrong idea.

So they ended up on the sofa, poring over pictures of Prague while their mugs of coffee cooled on the low table in front of them. The pictures were gorgeous—

soaring cathedrals, fairy-tale castles, steep-roofed houses, a horse and carriage in the snow...

'It's so old world and so very civilised,' Zoe said.

'I know. I couldn't think of any place more different from Queensland.'

'I can't believe I'm going to see it all. I'm booked into a small hotel just around the corner from the Old Town Square.'

Kent was silent for a bit. Frowning, he said, 'I hope you won't be too lonely spending Christmas overseas on your own.'

Zoe wondered if he was teasing her, but he looked quite genuine, and if she was honest she *was* a little worried about being on her own. But now with Bella unavailable it was a matter of travelling solo, or not at all. She looked sideways to find Kent still watching her with a troubled expression.

'I'll be fine,' she said. 'I've been doing some research, and, from what I've read, solo travellers have a much better chance of meeting people. There's always someone to share a meal or a bus ride.'

'I dare say that's true.' Kent picked up her hand and turned it over.

At the unexpected contact, Zoe's breath hitched and her heart picked up pace. 'What are you doing?'

'I'm reading your palm,' he said calmly.

She should have resisted, should have pulled her hand away, but it was already too late. She was mesmerised by his touch, by the scent of his aftershave, by the inescapable fabulousness of having him so close beside her.

Instead of protesting, she found herself playing his game. 'And what do you see in my palm?'

His eyes sparkled. 'Travel to far away places.'

'Fancy that. How perceptive.'

'And romance.'

Her palm curled instinctively. The warmth of his hands and the mellow teasing in his voice wove silken threads of longing deep inside her.

Fighting the hot urges, she challenged him. 'I thought palm readings only told you how long you're going to live and how many children you'll have.'

Kent's eyebrows lifted. 'Is that right? I'd better take another look, then.'

OK…she really should stop this nonsense. She tried to pull her hand away, but Kent was holding her firmly.

'Yes, of course,' he said. 'I can see a very long and happy life here.' With his forefinger he traced a shiver-sweet line across the centre of her palm. 'And a whole tribe of children.'

'A tribe?' Her breathlessness was caused more by his touch than his words. 'How many children are in a tribe?'

'Oh, I'd say around ten or eleven.'

'Far out.' Zoe tried to sound appalled, but she spoiled it by laughing. 'I think you'd better give up reading palms and stick to farming.'

Sure that her face was glowing bright pink, she switched her attention back to the book, still lying in her lap. It was open at a double page, showing Prague in the soft blue light of dusk. Four beautiful, ancient bridges spanned the Vltava River, and the sky and the water and the distant hills were all the exact same shade of misty blue. Even the splashes of yellow from street-lights and windows were soft and fuzzy. So pretty.

'Willara Downs is as lovely as this at dusk,' she told Kent.

To her surprise, he closed the book and set it on the

coffee table, then he took her hands, enclosing them in both of his. 'Zoe, I have a confession to make.'

Her heart skidded as if she'd taken a curve too fast.

'Would you be shocked if I told you that I fancied you *before* Bella and I called off the wedding?'

'Yes.' Of course she was shocked. Her heart was thumping so hard, she could hardly hear her own voice.

'Believe me, I was shocked, too. But I couldn't shut off my feelings.'

'But you didn't—' She pressed a hand to her thumping heart. She was scared and excited. Confused. 'You didn't call off the wedding because of me.'

'No, I didn't.' Smiling, Kent tucked a strand of her hair behind her ear. 'You don't have to feel guilty. It was only afterwards that I allowed myself to think about what had been happening. By then, I realised that I fancied you like crazy.'

She closed her eyes, searching for the strength to resist him. Kent had fancied lots of girls. This wasn't a confession of love. But even though she knew this, his words were unfurling fiery ribbons of need inside her. His touch was clouding her thoughts.

When his thumb brushed gently over her lips, she couldn't think of anything but kissing him again, of throwing herself into his wonderful, strong arms, of climbing brazenly into his lap…the bliss of skin against skin…

'You're lovely,' he whispered.

'Kent, don't say that.' She dragged herself back from the magnetic pull of his touch. 'You mustn't. We can't.'

'Why can't we?'

Remember Rodney.

But Kent was nothing like Rodney. He wasn't up and down in his moods as Rodney had been. He'd been engaged to Bella for noble reasons and he'd been very considerate of everyone's feelings when he'd broken that commitment. He was a man who took responsibilities seriously.

Even so, by his own confession, he still wasn't the marrying and settling down type.

Maybe I can simply enjoy the moment?

In a few weeks she was going to Europe, and Kent knew that, so a liaison now could only be temporary. Temporary flings were safe. They couldn't break a girl's heart. She could look on her trip overseas as her escape route.

Besides…heaven help her, she wanted this man… wanted him to kiss her, wanted his kiss so badly she was trembling. Every nerve in her body was quivering.

Kent dipped his head till his lips were almost touching hers. She looked into his eyes and saw the dark urgency of her longing mirrored there. A soft gasp escaped her, an embarrassing, pleading sound.

His mouth brushed hers, slow but insistent. 'Tell me why this is wrong,' he murmured against her lips.

She couldn't answer. If there had ever been a reason to say no, she'd lost it. His lips caressed hers again, and the last warnings in her head crumpled like tissue paper thrown on fire. She couldn't think of anything but returning Kent's kiss. Already she was winding her arms around his neck…and she kissed him.

Kissed him and *kissed* him.

Somewhere in the midst of kissing him, she kicked off her shoes and wriggled into his lap. And this time it was he who gasped. Then his hands traced the silky shape of her legs encased in tights. He dropped a fiery line of kisses over her skin from her collarbone into the V of her blouse. Then their mouths met again, and

their kisses turned molten as they tumbled sideways—
a blissful tangle into the deep red cushions.

Out of habit, Kent woke early, but this morning, instead
of bouncing out to face a day's farm work, he lay in the
soft light watching Zoe sleep. She was on her side, facing him, her dark hair tumbling over the white pillow,
her dusky eyelashes curving against her soft cheeks, her
mouth pale and slightly open. She looked so innocent
and vulnerable now, so different from the fiery, sensuous woman who'd made love to him last night.

Last night…

When he'd knocked on Zoe's door, he hadn't known
what to expect. Hadn't dared to hope that he might end
up spending the night with her. And yet, he couldn't
deny he'd been on fire since their farewell kiss at
Willara.

Even so, last night had defied all logic. He and Zoe
had shared a mere explosion of passion and excitement,
but there'd been astonishing tenderness, too. The same
kind of emotional connection he'd felt before—over
dinner conversations or on the creek bank. An amazing sense of rightness. A certainty that some kind of
miracle had been set in motion.

Briefly, as he lay there, he wondered if such thoughts
were fanciful. But then Zoe stirred beside him, opened
her bright blue eyes and smiled, and he was flooded
with a wonderful sense of buoyancy. Perhaps his life
was taking a turn in a very good direction.

CHAPTER TEN

ZOE's new version of heaven was waking up beside Kent Rigby on a Saturday morning and knowing they had the whole, delicious weekend to spend together.

They rose late, and went out to have breakfast at a pavement café that served great coffee and luscious, tasty mushrooms on thick sourdough toast. Afterwards, they walked beneath flowering jacarandas on the banks of the Brisbane River, enjoying the sunshine, and sharing happy, goofy smiles.

In the afternoon they went to a suburban cinema to see a creepy thriller movie. Like teenagers they stole popcorn flavoured kisses in the dark, and on the way home they stopped off at a supermarket and bought ingredients for a pasta dish to make at home.

In Zoe's kitchen they sipped wine while they chopped and cooked. Every chance they had, they touched and smiled and hugged and kissed. They were, in a word, entranced.

Wrapped in a bubble of bliss, Zoe wouldn't let anything intrude. No negative thoughts, no questions, no doubts. If the slightest misgiving about history repeating itself reared its ugly head, she told herself this time was nothing like her disaster with Rodney. Rodney had moved in. Rodney had promised for ever.

With Kent, she was merely enjoying a fab weekend. At the end of two days he would go back to Willara, knowing that she was about to leave for overseas. For now she was trusting her instincts and her instincts felt *fantastic*!

Their pasta sauce was bubbling beautifully and Kent was stealing yet another kiss from Zoe when the phone rang. She grabbed the receiver and trilled 'Hello-o-o,' in a super-happy singsong.

'Zoe, how are you?'

'Bella?' Zoe shot a startled glance to Kent and watched his eyebrows hike.

Bella laughed. 'Don't sound so surprised.'

'Sorry. I wasn't expecting you, Bella, and I was—um—distracted for a moment.'

'Are you all right, Zoe?'

'Absolutely fine. Why?'

'I don't know. You sound—different somehow.'

'I don't think I'm different. More importantly, how are you?' Zoe flashed another glance Kent's way.

His eyes were more cautious now, as if he felt as awkward as she did. It would be so hard to explain this to Bella. A week ago, Zoe had been focused on being the perfect bridesmaid. Last night she'd slept with the bridegroom. Admittedly, those roles were now defunct, but how would Bella react if she knew they were together so soon?

And just like that, with Bella on the other end of the line, Zoe saw her wonderful weekend in a whole new light—as an outsider might—and her brain flung up words like *impetuous, cheeky, reckless...*

Bella said, 'I'm fine, thanks. I'm in Port Douglas with our grandparents. There's been a cyclone, would you believe? But we're all OK. Just garden damage.'

'That's really bad luck about the cyclone. How's everything…going…with…Damon?'

'OK,' Bella said in a sharp, *don't-go-there* tone. 'I was actually ringing to see if you've been in touch with Kent.'

'Oh?' Zoe was instantly nervous. She widened her eyes at Kent. Pointing to the phone, she mouthed, *'Do you want to talk to Bella?'*

Frowning, he shook his head.

She swallowed. 'Yes, I've had *some* contact with him.'

'I tried his mobile, but he's switched it off, so I rang the homestead and he wasn't there either so I rang his parents and Stephanie told me he's away for the weekend.'

'Did you want Kent for anything important?'

'Not especially. I guess I just wanted to make sure he's OK. You know the wedding would have been happening right about now.'

Oh, gosh. Zoe glanced at the clock on her kitchen wall and saw that Bella was right. At this very moment, Bella and Kent should have been exchanging their marriage vows. How on earth had it slipped her mind?

'I would have liked to make certain that Kent was OK,' Bella said.

'I'm sure he's fine. He's probably decided not to dwell on the wedding too much.'

'Yes, that would be best, wouldn't it? I hope you're right.'

On the stove the sauce began to boil and spit. Zoe gestured frantically, but Kent had moved to the window and was standing with his back to her, studiously looking out into her backyard. His shoulders were squared and his back very straight. Sure signs of tension.

Zoe tried to attract him with a stage whisper. *'Pssst, can you turn that sauce down?'*

'Do you have someone there?' Bella asked.

'Yes—just—a friend over for dinner.'

'Oh, that's nice. I won't keep you, then.' But instead of hanging up, Bella lowered her voice. 'Would this friend be male by any chance?'

Zoe made the mistake of hesitating for a shade too long.

'Zoe, it's a guy, isn't it? That's why you sounded so different—sort of bubbly and excited. Who is he? Anyone I know?'

'Bell, I'm sorry. The dinner's burning, and I've got to go. But it's been fantastic to hear from you and to know you're OK.'

'All right.' Bella laughed. 'I can take a hint. But if you hear from Kent, tell him that I rang and, apart from the weather, I'm fine.'

'I will, and I'll tell him you were thinking of him.'

Zoe hung up and rushed to rescue the sauce. Kent turned from the window, and she sank back against a cupboard, letting out a groan. 'That was awful. I felt terrible lying to her.'

'You weren't exactly lying.'

'No, but I was hiding the truth and that's just as bad.'

Zoe felt sick. Hands clenched, she paced across the kitchen. And to her horror, all the reasons she shouldn't be with Kent rushed back to taunt her. What was she doing leaping into bed with another man who'd just broken off an engagement?

Spinning around, she challenged him. 'Had you remembered that you should have been getting married right now?'

He looked uncomfortable. 'Is that why Bella rang?'

'Yes. She was worried about you. She tried the Willara Downs number and your mobile.'

Pulling his phone from his pocket, Kent thumbed a button or two. 'It's not that I don't want to talk to her. I didn't want to embarrass you. I'll call her back now.'

'Actually…I'm not sure that's a good idea. If you call back straight away, she'll probably guess you're with me. She's already figured I have a guy here.'

Grimacing, Kent stood looking down at the phone. It looked tiny in his big brown work-roughened hand. His throat rippled as he swallowed. 'I'm sure Bella will understand if I explain.'

Zoe gave a choked laugh. 'How are you going to explain that you ended up spending the weekend with her bridesmaid? It'll sound so—' she swallowed, grasping for a word '—tacky.'

'Tacky?' Kent repeated, shocked.

'Hasty, then. Indecently so.'

In two steps, Kent was across the room and grabbing Zoe's arm. 'Is that what you think? That last night was tacky?'

'No.' Suddenly, Zoe was trembling and fighting tears. 'Oh, Kent, you have to admit it might be viewed by many as indecent haste.'

He pulled her in to him, holding her against his broad chest, kissing her hair. 'Whatever's happening between us is *good*.' Gently, he tucked her hair behind her ear and kissed her brow. 'And it's no one else's business.'

Zoe closed her eyes and let her head sink against his shoulder. She loved being with this man so much— loved the way he smelled of sunlight and clean shirts, loved the hard strength of his body, and the warm reassurance of his arms wrapped around her. Loved who he was.

But she had loved Rodney, too. She'd adored him. She could never have believed he might hurt her.

'How did we let this happen so soon?' she asked Kent.

For answer, he hugged her closer, but even as warmth and pleasure seeped through her the impact of Bella's phone call remained, lifting the lid on all the difficult questions she'd doggedly resisted for the past twenty-four hours. And one thing was certain—she couldn't find answers to these questions while she was in Kent's arms.

With enormous reluctance she pulled away, went to the window and opened it, letting in a fresh breeze as if, somehow, that might clear her thoughts.

'I never meant this to happen,' she said. 'After that kiss goodbye last weekend I decided we shouldn't get too involved. It's all too soon. Too convenient.'

She looked down at her hands—rubbed the rough edge of a thumbnail. The real issue here was that Kent didn't want to settle down. He'd said so last night. She, on the other hand, wanted nothing more than to marry and start a family—to be the bride, not the bridesmaid. And Kent was exactly the sort of man... No, he was the *only* man she wanted to settle down with.

She couldn't tell him that. There was no point. 'I can't help worrying that this weekend has been a mistake,' she said instead.

'You mean you're feeling pressured?'

'Well, yes. I tried to tell you last night that we shouldn't...' She shot him an accusing glance. 'I'm sure you remember.'

'Oh, yes, I remember.' Kent's slow smile made her wince.

No doubt he was remembering the way she'd shamelessly climbed into his lap and kissed him as if there were no tomorrow. She was so hopelessly weak around him and last night she'd foolishly given in to that weakness.

Now she was determined to be strong. 'The thing is, I've been through something like this before, Kent.'

He frowned. 'How do you mean?'

'I fell for a guy who'd recently broken off an engagement. He was a work colleague and I'd known him for about twelve months. I'd even met his fiancée, Naomi, at parties. A few months after their break-up he asked me out, and I conscientiously tried to cheer him up. All went well. He moved in with me and we lived together for another six months. Until—'

Zoe paused for dramatic emphasis.

'Until he let you down,' Kent suggested.

'Yes. I came home one Friday evening and found him in *my* bed with Naomi.'

He scowled. 'That's a low-down act.'

'That's why I call him Rodney the Rat.' Zoe closed her eyes at the memory. 'He made me feel used and stupid and conned and hurt and angry. You name it—I felt it. I was devastated.'

And now…she wouldn't run the risk of being hurt again, surely? She'd been a fool to let herself fall for Kent so quickly and easily, when she'd spent the past week telling herself that it wasn't wise.

'Zoe, I swear I would never do anything to you like that.'

'I know you wouldn't hurt me intentionally, but I can't help feeling vulnerable.' Impatiently, she swept a lock of hair from her eyes. 'Maybe I'm jumping the gun. We haven't even talked about what we want from—from this. Are we having a fling—or—or—?'

'I thought we were getting to know each other.' He came to stand beside her again, and with his hands on her shoulders he turned her to look at him, trapping her with the dark, frank depths of his eyes. 'We were honest with each other when we made love, weren't we?'

Zoe couldn't deny there'd been a special openness and sincerity about last night. But that was the problem. To her, it had felt like so much more than a temporary fling and just thinking about it brought her to the edge of tears.

She took a deep breath. If she played this the wrong way, she would lose Kent, and live to regret it deeply. But her bigger fear was that she'd keep seeing him for several more weeks and *then* the novelty would wear off for him. To spend more time with him and then lose him would be so much worse. Unbearable.

The hard truth was that every moment she spent with Kent was dangerous. She'd been falling more deeply in love with him since the moment she'd met him beside the road side. If she didn't apply the brakes now, before she was in any deeper, she could end up *very* badly hurt. Again.

It was important now to list her extremely valid concerns.

'Kent, until last weekend, you were all set to marry my best friend. You were ready to vow to love her till you were parted by death.'

A muscle jerked in his jaw. 'But you know why we called it off.'

'Yes, I do. And I can understand why you want to move on with your life. But I'm not sure it's a great idea to move straight on to the bridesmaid, as if I was there, ready and waiting—like the next cab on the rank.'

Zoe knew it was a cheap shot, and a sound like a

growl broke from him. Anger flashed in his eyes and he looked so unlike his calm, easy-going self that she almost backed down and apologised. But then where would she be? In his arms with nothing sorted? Nothing solved?

Kent's eyes narrowed. 'Are you asking me to leave?'

No, no, no. That wasn't what she wanted at all. How could she let him go? She'd been so looking forward to this evening—to their shared meal, and the long night after—and then, all of Sunday still ahead of them. And their future…

She dropped her gaze to the floor. It was too hard to think when Kent was standing right there all gorgeous and frowning in front of her.

Be strong, Zoe.

She took a deep breath before she spoke. 'Perhaps we just need space to sort things out—a sort of cooling-off period.' She hoped she didn't sound as miserable as she felt.

Kent remained very still, and his dark eyes, usually so warm and sparkling, remained severe and narrowed. 'Cooling-off period? So what's that? Forty-eight hours? Four weeks?'

I don't know! she wanted to wail.

Kent, however, had made his decision. 'It's clear I should go.' Stepping forward, he dropped a light kiss on her cheek. 'I'll be in touch, then.' And just like that, he was heading out of her kitchen.

Zoe wanted to call him back.

Don't you want dinner? It's a long drive back to Willara. She shot a desperate glance to the sauce-spattered stove. They'd cooked all this pasta.

But what about your things? she almost called out, until she remembered that Kent hadn't brought any luggage. He'd slept naked, and used her spare toothbrush—because he hadn't planned to stay…

Everything that had happened this weekend had been wonderfully spontaneous and…

And now she'd spoiled it.

Stumbling behind him through the flat, she swiped at embarrassing tears. When they reached her front door, Kent turned to her again, looking so desperately stern and handsome Zoe could barely breathe.

'I guess I need to get this straight,' he said. 'While we're cooling off, what exactly are we sorting out?'

Zoe gulped. Her mind was swirling. What could she say? Was this the time for painful honesty? What else could she offer him? 'I'm worried that I'm not the right girl for you, Kent.'

He stood, wary-eyed, waiting for her to continue.

Now that she'd started, she had no choice but to confess. 'I'm afraid I'm very keen on you, keener than you realise. And I don't think you'd want to deal with that right now.' Taking a deep breath, she rushed on. 'To be honest, I'm in love with the whole picture of you and your farm and your country lifestyle.'

Kent didn't speak. Perhaps he was stunned, or simply puzzled.

And Zoe realised, now, too late, that it had been a mistake to mention any of this, but she felt compelled to explain. 'It started when I was little, living in a bus and always looking out of the window at snug farmhouses in the middle of neat, tidy fields. I thought they looked so wonderful and I developed this fantasy of marrying a farmer one day.'

'So I'm a fantasy?' he queried, looking uncomfortable. 'Along with a country wedding?'

Oh, God. Too much information.

'I'm making a hash of this,' Zoe said. 'I didn't mean that the only reason I like you is because you're a farmer.'

'OK.' He lifted a hand as if to put a stop to the conversation. 'This is getting way too complicated.'

'I'm sorry.'

'Don't apologise, but I take your point about a cooling-off period. I guess it's a good idea.'

Thud. It was ridiculous to be disappointed as soon as he agreed to the very thing she'd asked for. Zoe's throat was suddenly a scalding knot of unshed tears.

Already he was turning to leave, but she couldn't speak, was too busy keeping her lips pressed together to hold back embarrassing sobs.

'Take care,' he said gently, before he went swiftly down her steps to his ute.

Driving west against the fierce glare of the setting sun, Kent had never felt less like cooling off.

He was fired up. Burning.

Angry with himself.

Last week he'd been a step from marrying Zoe's best friend, and a week later he'd leapt straight into her bed. What was he thinking?

Of course it was a hasty, rash and thoughtless act. If one of his mates had behaved the same way, Kent would be wondering if the guy's actions were driven by a bruised ego, or by his brains dropping below his belt!

Zoe had every right to ask questions—questions he should have asked himself.

What did he want from this relationship? Was it a casual fling? Did he expect to follow his old pattern, to date her for a month or so, and then drift away?

He certainly hadn't been thinking about the long term.

After last week's close brush with the responsibility and permanence of matrimony, he'd been set free, so to speak. He was free to embrace his old ways and his plan was to prolong his bachelorhood for as long as he could.

But did he honestly expect a conscientious girl like Zoe to treat their relationship lightly? After her past weeks of hard work and dedication, shouldn't he have known better? After she'd made love with such breath-taking spontaneity and touching emotion, shouldn't he have known their liaison was already complicated?

Hell. Zoe had told him about her rat of a boyfriend, and he'd been so self-righteous.

I would never do anything to you like that. What a fool he was.

Selfish, too. He'd wanted a little fun after the tension and drama of the past weeks, and Zoe had been available. How had she put it? The next cab at the rank.

And yet—that wasn't how he thought of her. Zoe was special, amazing in so many ways—the kind of girl he could, quite possibly, marry one day…if he'd had plans to settle down.

Maybe he shouldn't have been so surprised by her confession that she had feelings for him and wanted to marry, that she'd always wanted to be a farmer's wife, for heaven's sake.

But he hadn't seen it coming, and now, instead of relaxing after a pleasant weekend, he had a lot to think about. Too much. Not a chance of cooling off.

CHAPTER ELEVEN

It was ten-thirty when the delivery boy arrived at the office doorway. At least, Zoe assumed it was the delivery boy, although all she could see of him were his jeans and his grubby green and yellow sneakers. The top half of him was entirely obscured by the biggest bunch of flowers she'd ever seen.

As the flowers appeared there was a collective gasp from every female in the office. The girl at the desk nearest to Zoe stopped a phone conversation in mid-sentence. Someone else gave an excited little squeal.

Mandy, whose desk was closest to the door, got out of her seat and practically tiptoed in awe towards the mountain of blooms.

Zoe was as curious as anyone else as she exchanged smiles with her workmates. She knew everyone was trying to guess who the lucky recipient could be. Emily had recently announced she was pregnant. Joanne was turning forty soon. Jane had acquired a new and, apparently, ultra-romantic boyfriend.

At least, Zoe knew the flowers couldn't be for her. The only person who might send them was Kent and he'd embraced her cooling-off suggestion with depressing enthusiasm. It was three weeks now since she'd seen him. Three desperately miserable weeks.

In all that time, she'd made no attempt to contact him and he'd only been in touch once to report that, despite the terrible weather in the north, Bella and Damon were apparently OK. There'd been nothing personal in his message. Not a breath of romance.

The silence had been awful. At times Zoe had felt so miserable, she'd almost weakened and begged him to forget everything she'd said.

Fortunately, she'd restrained herself. She'd done enough damage last time when she'd talked about loving him. Of course she'd frightened him off.

If she'd handled everything sensibly, they would have continued to see each other on weekends and who knew what pleasing developments might have occurred?

Now, in just a few days, she would be leaving for Europe, so there was no point in even thinking about what might have been with Kent. Instead, she was hoping and praying that the exciting new foreign sights and experiences would cheer her up, and help her to put the whole Willara experience behind her.

At any rate, she could relax right now. There was absolutely no chance these flowers were for her.

At the doorway, the floral Mount Everest was handed over to Mandy, who had to turn sideways to see where she was going as she made her way carefully back into the centre of the office.

'Help, someone!' she called. 'I'm sure there's a card pinned on here, but I can't possibly reach it.'

Zoe jumped to assist her. The bouquet was so huge, it took a few moments to locate the small white envelope, but she finally found it pinned beneath a cascade of lavender orchids.

'Here!' she cried, triumphantly waving the small white envelope above her head like a trophy.

'Who's it for?' cried several voices.

All eyes in the room were on Zoe. She saw smiles of amusement, wistful faces filled with hope, others wide eyed with genuine tension. The air was shimmering with palpable excitement.

Suddenly the centre of attention, Zoe felt her heart-beats begin a drum roll as she deliberately took her time looking at the name on the envelope. Then she dropped her gaze to the white square of paper. And her heart stopped beating altogether.

There…on the envelope in clear blue ink…

Zoe Weston.

There was a painful thump in the centre of her chest, and then her heart began to pound savagely. She hadn't expected, hadn't dreamed… The paper in her hand was shaking.

Everyone was watching her.

'Oh, gosh.'

'Who's it for?' Mandy demanded.

Almost apologetically, Zoe said, 'Me.'

At first there was silence. Then a voice cried, 'Oh, wow! Congratulations!' But for Zoe this was almost drowned out by her thundering heartbeats.

Her hands were shaking so badly, she had a hard time getting the little card out of the envelope, but finally she was able to read it.

I'd like to talk. How about you?
Kent xx

A thrill burst inside her like fizzing champagne.

'Who's it from?' called Jane.

Zoe hesitated. Many of these girls had been to

Willara Downs for the bridal shower. 'Just a guy,' she said lamely. As you did.

The response was a predictable group groan.

'If a guy sends a bouquet the size of a house he must be asking you to marry him at the very least,' someone said.

'Or perhaps he's been a very, very bad boy and he's very, very sorry,' said someone else.

Zoe shook her head, but she wasn't about to tell them: *he just wants to talk*. She was still trembling as she took the flowers from Mandy and stumbled off to hunt for a bucket to put them in.

In a back room she found a metal waste-paper bin, and she filled it with water. With the flowers taken care of, she sank back against a filing cabinet and read Kent's note again.

I'd like to talk. How about you?

Every possible emotion raged war inside her. Joy. Hope. Fear. Uncertainty.

Kent was opening a door, trying to reconnect, and she couldn't think of anything she wanted more than to see him again.

But in a few days she would be flying to the other side of the world, and she'd be away for a month. Surely her sudden impatience to see him was foolish.

Just because he's sent me a bunch of flowers?

But I love him.

Did she? Really?

She'd had enough time to think about it, to try to work out if she was actually in love with the real man and not with an embodiment of her childhood fantasy.

She found herself asking how anyone ever knew for certain that they were truly in love. In three weeks her longing to see Kent had been agonising. Was that love?

Was love ever safe and certain, or was it always a great big gamble?

She reminded herself again, as she had so often in the past three weeks, of her headlong rush into love with Rodney. She'd been so certain he was The One.

She'd been such a diligent girlfriend, so anxious to please Rodney, cooking his favourite meals, hiring his favourite DVDs. She'd been so busy showing him how devoted she was, she'd never stopped to make sure he felt the same way.

Being dumped by him had awoken every one of her insecurities. Once again she'd been an outsider, without a best mate.

Lately, she'd even wondered if she had poor judgement when it came to men. Perhaps it would be much more sensible to wait to talk to Kent after she got back from her travels. Mightn't she gain a clearer perspective with the benefit of further time and distance?

At lunchtime, Zoe divided the flowers into smaller bunches and handed them out among her surprised work colleagues.

'There's no point in taking them home to my place,' she explained over and over. 'I'm leaving for Europe on the weekend. You may as well enjoy them.'

The only flowers Zoe saved were the lavender orchids, which she took home and placed in a vase on the shelf beside the fish tank.

That was the easy part. Deciding how to deal with Kent was the difficult bit. She had to ring him to thank him, and there shouldn't be any harm in a phone call. Just the same, she had to be careful not to say too much. Now, when she was about to leave, she certainly couldn't let on how much she'd missed him.

No, she would have to be very strong and in control

of this conversation. Most definitely, she mustn't allow Kent to say or do anything to spoil her holiday plans.

The phone's shrill ring sent a jolt of adrenalin punching into Kent. He willed himself to stay calm. Almost certainly, this would be yet another phone call from a wedding guest, calling to cheer him up, or to invite him over for a meal. There'd been many such calls during the past month.

Even so, Kent knew the flowers must have arrived in Brisbane, and he was picturing Zoe as he picked up the receiver. He imagined her on her sofa in her Newmarket flat, with her long legs tucked neatly beneath her, her shiny hair a dark splash against the vivid red of her sofa's upholstery. Her eyes the blue of the morning sky…

He forced a smile into his voice as he answered. 'Hello. Willara Downs.'

'Hi, Kent, it's Zoe.'

Twin reactions—elation and alarm—tightened like lassos around his chest. It was so good to hear her voice and he couldn't believe how much he'd missed her. For these past three weeks he'd spent far too much time thinking about her, missing her smile, her touch, her company.

But he couldn't believe how worried he was, too. Worried she would read too much into this gesture. He simply needed to see her again. From their first meeting, he'd been aware of a fatal chemistry, and he'd tried his best to ignore it, but it was still tormenting him like a constant ache.

He'd given in, sent the flowers and a request to make contact, and now he forced a smile into his voice. 'Hey, Zoe, it's great to hear from you. How are you?'

'I'm fine, thanks.'

She didn't sound fine. She sounded nervous, as nervous as he was.

'Your flowers arrived,' she said. 'Thank you so much, Kent. They're beautiful. There were so many of them.'

'Not too over the top, I hope. I ordered them over the phone and just named an amount. Anyway, I'm glad you liked them.'

'All the girls in the office were jealous.' After a small pause, she asked, 'How—how are you?'

'Fighting fit.' He swallowed a sudden constriction in his throat. 'But I've missed you, Zoe.'

'Oh.'

Oh? What was that supposed to mean? He needed to know if she was pleased or disappointed. 'I was wondering if you'd had enough of this cooling-off period.'

'It hasn't been much fun,' she said softly, but then added almost straight away, 'but I still think it's a sensible idea, don't you?'

'I'm not sure it's possible to sort out a relationship in isolation. I was hoping we could talk.'

She made a noise that sounded like a sigh. A sad sigh that chilled him. 'I'm leaving for Europe on Saturday, Kent.'

'So soon? But Christmas is a month away.'

'I'm going to London and Paris first. Ten days in each city, and then on to Prague.'

A curse fell from his lips before he could bite it back. He didn't want to wait another month. He'd had enough of waiting while his thoughts went round and round the same worn track. Solitary contemplation hadn't helped.

He couldn't make decisions about their relationship in a vacuum.

He wanted action. He needed to be able to touch Zoe, to share meals and conversations, to make love to her.

If they waited another month, Zoe would have all kinds of opportunities to meet suave, silver-tongued Continental Casanovas. Hell. Had she already dismissed him?

Surely she owed him another chance? He had to see her. 'I'll come down to Brisbane.' Kent glanced at his watch. It was too late tonight. 'How about tomorrow night?'

'Sorry, Kent, my parents will be here. They're coming up to Brisbane to collect the goldfish and my pot plants.'

Curse the goldfish. Why had he ever thought it was a good idea? 'What about Friday night, then?'

There was another, longer pause. 'I—I'm not sure that's a good idea. I'll be leaving early on Saturday morning. Maybe we should let this go till I get back.'

'Sorry, Zoe. That's not an option. I have to see you. I'll come to the airport. What's your flight number?'

'Honestly, there's no need to see me off.'

'You can't keep stalling.' He was bulldozing her, but he didn't care. He'd heard a quiver in her voice that hinted at her inner battle, and in that instant he'd decided there was no way he could let her leave for the far side of the world without seeing her.

'Just tell me the flight and I'll be there.'

'OK, but I'll need to make a condition though, Kent.'

'What is it?'

'Promise you won't try to talk me out of going away.'

'Agreed,' he said, with a reluctance that disturbed him.

* * *

Zoe's boarding pass was tucked into her handbag and her suitcase was already on its way down the conveyor belt as she scanned the international terminal, searching for Kent.

Despite her best efforts to remain calm, her insides were flapping like bait in a net. She couldn't wait to see him, couldn't believe he was driving all the way from Willara Downs to Brisbane airport to spend a few short minutes with her.

How amazing was that? She'd given him a chance to cool off and it seemed that he hadn't cooled.

Of course, she hadn't cooled either. She was desperate to see him. And yet she was scared. For three and a half weeks, she'd kept her feelings for Kent carefully tied up in tight little parcels, and now, when she was about to head overseas, she wanted them to stay that way.

This trip was important to her. She was looking forward to the exciting new sights and sounds and smells of foreign places.

More importantly, she was hoping that time and distance would offer her an excellent chance to sort through her emotions and get a new perspective on her hopes and dreams. It would give Kent time, too.

Right now, however, she was scared. Scared that seeing him again would unravel her tightly bound feelings. Scared that one look into the deep brown warmth in his eyes could too easily break her resolve. How awful if her emotions spilled out all over the airport, like luggage bursting from an over-stuffed suitcase.

I can't let that happen. I have to be strong.

It would be so much easier to leave now without seeing him. All she had to do was walk through the exit doors into the secure Customs area and Kent wouldn't be able to follow her. Then she could keep herself together until she was safely out of reach. Should she leave? Now?

'Zoe.'

His voice came from behind her, spinning her around, a smile already flooding her face.

Oh, wow! He looked even more wonderful than she'd remembered. He was so tall and broad shouldered and his skin was darker, as if he'd spent a lot of time outdoors.

They stood, just staring at each other. Not touching.

'I'm late,' he said. 'The traffic was insane. I was afraid I'd miss you.'

'It won't be long before I have to go.'

'That's OK. At least I'm here now.' He smiled.

Heavens, his smile was gorgeous.

Dangerous. Zoe wanted to lean in to him, to touch him, to smell him.

Instead she searched for safe conversation. 'How's everything on the farm?'

'All running along smoothly.'

'Who's looking after the garden?'

Kent smiled again, but his eyes were watching her with hawklike attention. 'I have my work cut out running the farm, and my mother's busy planting up her new cottage garden, so, for now, the garden's looking after itself.'

'That's a shame.' There would be so many weeds, and the roses would need dead-heading. All the lilies and irises would be out now, but there'd be no one to truly appreciate them.

'I might get someone in,' he said, still watching her.

Zoe nodded and told herself to forget Willara Downs.

Kent said, 'You're going to have a fabulous trip.'

She was grateful that he wasn't going to try to stop her from leaving. She hoped he had no idea how easily he could.

His eyes searched her face, again, worried now. 'You'll be careful, won't you, Zoe?'

'Of course. Don't worry. My dad's given me all the lectures about a girl overseas on her own… I have a long list of instructions. Use a money belt. Keep enough money for the day in my pocket. Stay away from the lonely spots.'

'All very good advice.'

'And I've scanned my travel documents and emailed them to myself.'

'Great. And remember to keep in touch,' Kent added.

'That, too.' She smiled. 'I have international texting on my mobile phone.'

'And you have my number, I hope.'

'Yes. I'll text you.'

'Promise?'

The dark intensity in his eyes made her heart stumble. 'I promise, Kent.'

His shoulders visibly relaxed, and it was only then that she realised how very tense he'd been. 'Text me as often as you like, Zoe. If you're having a great time, or—or a not so great time.'

'I will.' She smiled. 'Don't look so worried.'

'I can't help it. I'm letting you go.'

She didn't know what to say. She hadn't expected him to be quite so…so protective…and she was scared she'd start to cry. 'I should head off now.'

He touched her elbow. 'You can't rush off without a decent goodbye.'

It was a warning, Zoe realised, not a request. But

Kent gave her no chance to deny him. In a heartbeat, he'd gathered her in, and he was kissing her.

Not hungrily, as she might have expected after their three-week stand-off, but with devastating tenderness. And heaven help her, she couldn't even pretend to resist. He only had to touch her and her will power evaporated like mist in sunlight.

Now, he'd barely sipped at her lower lip and, already, she was trembling.

His lips brushed her top lip. A kiss, as teasing and as light as air. Heartbreaking in its sexiness. He pressed another kiss to the corner of her mouth.

Wherever his lips touched her, Zoe melted.

Her knees threatened to give away as he took the kiss dizzyingly deeper, and she had no choice but to cling to him, grabbing handfuls of his T-shirt to steady herself. Now she was truly melting all over. Melting from head to toe. Dissolving right there. In the busy airport.

The bustling crowds and the voices over the intercom faded as Zoe became lost in the deep, dark mystery of Kent's kiss. Her impending flight no longer mattered. The whole world was happening right here. In Kent's arms.

When he released her, she wanted to cry.

Gently, he tucked a strand of her hair behind her ear, and his eyes betrayed a mix of sadness and triumph. 'So, Zoe…about this cooling-off idea.'

Right now, the cooling off was quite obviously the most ridiculous idea she'd ever had.

Then again, this kiss only proved how very badly she needed a safety net. She was so susceptible to this man. She lost her head whenever he was near. His kisses made her want to cancel her flight, tear up her ticket and toss her passport in the nearest waste bin.

Snap out of it, Zoe. For heaven's sake pull yourself together. Now.

She squared her shoulders. 'I—I don't think we should change our current status before I get back.'

Kent was smiling, damn him. 'So I guess this fare-well kiss was an exception.'

Somehow, miraculously, Zoe kept her face poker straight. 'Under the circumstances, it was an excus-able infringement.' With deliberate brusqueness, she checked the time on her phone. 'I'm sorry. I really must go now.'

To her surprise, Kent nodded. 'Yes, you must. I hope you have a safe journey, Zoe.'

'Thanks.'

It was happening. Kent was letting her go. Why couldn't she feel relieved?

His eyes were burning and serious. 'Remember to stay in touch. Your messages can be as cool as you like, but keep them coming.'

'All right.'

She thought he might kiss her again. And he did. He dropped one last, sweet, too-tempting and too-brief kiss on her lips, and then he stepped away from her, his throat rippling.

He lifted his hand.

Zoe's vision blurred and when she tried to walk her shoes were filled with lead.

CHAPTER TWELVE

AT FIRST, Zoe managed quite well. In London and Paris there were so many famous sights she wanted to see, so many beautiful art galleries, and amazing, historic buildings. So many wonderfully enticing shops to explore. She managed to keep busy every day and she found each new experience thrilling and exciting.

She also discovered definite advantages to solo travelling—total freedom to decide what she wanted to see and where she should stay, or when and where she should eat. And she met lots of interesting fellow travellers from all over the world.

But of course, she missed Kent and thought of him often.

Too often.

No way could she pretend she didn't miss him. He was always there, as an ache beneath her breastbone, a tightness in her throat. Her solo travels would have been a thousand times better if he'd been there to share everything with her.

Even so, she was very disciplined. She restricted her text messages to Kent, allowing only one message every second day, and she kept them brief and cheerful. No mushy stuff.

Kent's responses were disappointing—often arriving much later than Zoe would have liked, even taking the time difference into consideration. And when he replied, his tone was cool and utterly lacking in anything even slightly mushy or romantic.

Clearly, he was taking her request to extend their cooling-off period seriously, and she knew she should be grateful for that. But there was always the chance that his interest in her was fading, just as she'd always feared.

Zoe hated how sick this thought made her.

She tried to cheer herself up by conjuring memories of their farewell kiss at the airport, but what an unhelpful exercise that was. She found herself missing Kent more and more every day.

It was dark when Kent got back to the homestead. He fed his dogs on the back veranda, then went into the kitchen to heat up a can of tomato soup for himself. He knew it was lazy, but it was already after eight, and he was too weary to bother about cooking a proper meal. Since Zoe left, he'd been working long hours, seven days a week, hoping that the self-imposed labour would act as a sedative.

It hadn't worked.

Nothing in his life felt right. Each night he fell into bed exhausted, but then couldn't sleep. His solitary existence, which had never bothered him before, was now suffocating.

He couldn't stop thinking about Zoe in Europe, wishing he were there. Worse, he kept reliving all the times they'd been together. Not just the lovemaking— all the everyday moments, like the evening she was here in his kitchen, making a salad while he flipped steaks, on another afternoon, preparing a roast, or sharing a sunset.

He remembered the meals they'd enjoyed on the back veranda, the conversations. Recalled Zoe's enthusiasm for the garden, remembered the morning she'd gone down to the creek with him to collect sand—the soft empathy in her eyes when she'd asked him about the accident.

Each small recollection had become painfully sharp and clear. So important.

Now that Kent had too much time to think, he realised that he'd been so caught up with the wedding plans that he'd never really noticed how perfectly Zoe fitted into life on Willara Downs. Now, despite his best attempts to ignore such dangerous thoughts, he knew that his plans for a lengthy bachelorhood were fast losing their charm.

It was not a comforting discovery. Small wonder he couldn't sleep.

For Zoe, things went from not so great to downright dismal when she arrived in Prague.

As her plane touched down she looked out at the banks of snow lining the cleared runway, and her first, her *only* thought was—*Kent should be here.*

Riding in the taxi from the airport, she couldn't stop thinking about him. She'd brought his beautiful book with her, and now the same gorgeous pictures she knew by heart were unfolding before her. She kept thinking about the night they'd shared dinner on the back veranda at Willara Downs, when Kent had first told her about Christmas in Prague.

If only he were here.

Impulsively, she sent him a text message.

1.30p.m.: I'm in Prague!!!!!!! My first glimpse of the fairy-tale skyline. Prague castle silhouetted against a winter-white sky. It stole my breath. So pretty and timeless.

She'd only come to Prague because Kent had told her about it, and now she was here, surrounded by its ancient, wintry beauty, she wanted him to be here with her. So badly. How could she enjoy the snow, the castles and the Christmas markets without him?

Loneliness descended like the snow.

She remembered all the overtures Kent had made before she left—the enormous bunch of flowers, the offers to visit her at her flat, the trip to the airport to say goodbye. Each time he'd tried to restart their relationship she'd blocked him.

Now, she had to ask why.

Why? *Why?*

Why had she been so fixated on keeping him at bay?

She was left with unanswered puzzles. She was surprised that he still seemed keen even though she'd spilled her dreams about settling down. Not that this meant he was ready to marry her. Perhaps he'd hoped to win her around to accepting a freer relationship. To Zoe, in her present lonely circumstances, that seemed to be a reasonable compromise.

However, her fixation with Kent annoyed her. She'd come away, hoping that distance and time would clear her head and her heart. But now, here she was in Prague on the far side of the world, and she still spent her whole time thinking about one man.

She missed his smile, missed his friendly brown eyes, the warmth and power of his arms about her. Missed his smell, his voice, his kisses, his touch...

And she had to ask why she'd insisted on an extension of their cooling off.

Her initial caution, so soon after the cancelled wedding, had been sensible. But was her request to continue it really such a good idea?

Suddenly, it made no sense to ration her text messages.

She had to make contact with Kent. If he couldn't be here, she needed to share her experiences by the only means she had. Opening her phone, she began to type.

4.15 p.m.: It's already dark and it's snowing and I'm wearing a new red woollen hat I bought in Paris.

5.45 p.m.: I'm in the Old Town Square. So many sounds. Church bells, a brass band playing carols, the chiming of the famous astronomical clock.

6.01 p.m.: Now I'm walking across Charles Bridge. There's a busker playing a violin. Magic.

7.10 p.m.: Goulash for dinner with five white dumplings to mop up the yummy rich beef gravy.

7.30 p.m.: Have just had my first drink of grog—a mix of rum and tea. Miss you heaps. Xx

By the time Zoe went to bed she'd had no reply from Kent. She told herself this was to be expected given the time differences, but it didn't stop her from feeling depressed and lonely and sorry for herself.

She knew it was pitiful, but she couldn't help feeling

down. She cried herself to sleep, and she slept fitfully, waking often to check her phone for messages.

There was only one, which arrived at 3.00 a.m. From her mum.

Next morning, Kent still hadn't replied, and Zoe found reasons—he'd risen early and taken off on his tractor without checking his phone. Or perhaps his phone's battery had needed recharging. She knew there were all sorts of logical explanations.

Just the same, she waited on tenterhooks. And to cheer herself up, she kept sending messages.

8.05 a.m.: From my apartment window, I look out at steep rooftops covered in snow and I can see Prague castle.

Don't you wish you were here?

8.35 a.m.: The cars are covered in snow. The statues have snow on their shoulders. The tree branches are sagging beneath the weight of the snow. There are children tobogganing.

What's it like at Willara?

9.15 a.m.: I'm trying to catch falling snow in my mouth. Can you tell snow's a novelty for me?

10.00 p.m.: Kent, I've been in Prague a whole day. Where are you?

At midnight, Zoe sat on her bed, wrapped in a warm quilt, staring forlornly at her phone. She'd written another message, but she wasn't quite brave enough to press Send. Kent's silence had made her desperate, but the message was so—*revealing*—and sending it was far too risky.

Heartsick, she read it again.

11.53 p.m.: Kent, I miss you so much. This cooling off isn't working any more. When I get back home, I hope we can talk.
I love you,
Zoe xxx

She'd changed the last part of the message a dozen times, had deleted and then rewritten those three telling words— *I love you.*

She knew this wasn't what he wanted to hear. How could she make such a rash confession? In the weeks since she'd left home, he hadn't given her any fresh reason to hope.

At twenty past midnight, Zoe was still huddled on the bed, but she decided she'd been too cautious for too long. What the heck? It was time to be brave.

Taking a deep breath for courage, she pressed the send button, and then she slipped beneath the covers, and tried to sleep. Her heart was pounding.

Next morning there was still no answer from Kent, and Zoe had never in her life felt as bereft as she did now.

She stood at the window looking out at the postcard-perfect scene of Europe's fairy-tale city. Overnight it had snowed again and all the rooftops and the streets were coated with glistening white. She didn't care. She didn't want to be in Prague. It was almost Christmas and she was alone and heartbroken and on the wrong side of the world.

How could she have been such a fool? How had she ever thought she could enjoy this alone?

But even if she paid the extra money to change her flights in the middle of the festive season, she didn't want to fly back to Australia if she couldn't be sure Kent would welcome her. That would be unbearable. Better to stay here in Prague and try to make the best of a bad situation.

She should try to put Kent out of her mind.

This morning she would go to the markets and buy Christmas decorations. She would school herself to live in each moment, to enjoy the ancient cobbled streets, and the old Gothic architecture, and the brightly decorated wooden huts selling handicrafts and wooden toys. Instead of dwelling on her misery, she would think of others. She would buy presents. Lots of presents. Her little brother, Toby, would love those cheeky wooden puppets.

But as Zoe walked from stall to stall she was painfully conscious of the small solid weight of her phone in her coat pocket. All morning, even though she knew it was the middle of the night in Australia, she remained on edge, waiting for the phone to vibrate against her hip, to tell her there was an incoming call.

In the afternoon, she joined a tour of Prague Castle and St Vitus Cathedral. The buildings were beautiful, and the history was epic and fascinating. The views of the city and the elegant bridges over the Vltava River were truly picturesque. Zoe soaked up the atmosphere and told herself how lucky she was to be having such memorable experiences. She told herself this over and over.

Her phone didn't ring.

By the time she'd finished the walking tour, darkness was closing in, but she didn't want to go back to her hotel room. She stayed out in the streets where the music and pretty lights were designed to lift everyone's spirits.

The air was thick with the warm smell of cinnamon and she admired the enormous, brightly lit Christmas tree which, according to the hotel concierge, had been brought down from the Sumava Mountains.

Every ten minutes or so, desperation drove her to take her phone out just to check that she hadn't missed a call.

She hadn't.

By now, her legs were leaden and aching from walking all day in the freezing cold. Her stomach was hollow with regret and self-recrimination. Her last message had been too strong. Kent didn't know how to answer her.

Or worse…

Kent had been in an accident. He was ill.

Stop it.

She would go mad if she kept this up. She should eat. The market stalls sold all kinds of wonderful hot food—corn on the cob, crumbed mushrooms and spicy sausages. Perhaps she should buy a cup of the hot mulled wine that everyone else seemed to be enjoying so much. The wine certainly looked and smelled yummy—spicy, with floating pieces of apple and orange.

At least it would keep her warm.

Slipping her phone into her coat pocket, Zoe gave it a small pat. Silently, she said: *That's it—I'm done with you for tonight.*

The thought was barely completed before she felt, through the soft kid of her glove, a gentle vibration against her fingers.

Her heart banged hard against her ribs. And then her phone began to ring in earnest.

This wasn't a mere text message. On the tiny screen she saw a name.

Kent Rigby...

Her hand was shaking as she held the phone to her ear.

Kent said, 'Zoe—'

And at that very moment a brass band struck up a noisy rendition of 'Good King Wenceslas', drowning out Kent's voice as it blasted the carol into the frosty night air.

'Sorry,' Zoe cried to him, running across the cobblestones with the phone pressed to one ear and her hand covering the other. 'I can't hear you. Hang on, Kent. Are you still there? I'm going to have to get away from this music.'

Around a corner, in a small, narrow street, she sank against a stone wall. 'Sorry,' she puffed. 'That's a little better. Are you still there?'

'Yes, I'm here.' His voice was rippling with warmth and a hint of laughter.

'Are you OK? It seems ages since I heard from you.'

'I'm fine, Zoe. How are you?'

'I'm OK. Everything's lovely here. But it's so good to hear your voice.'

'Are you homesick?'

'I am a bit, yes.' Nervously, she chewed her lip. 'Have my text messages been getting through to you?'

'They have.' There was a tiny pause. 'Thank you.' His voice sounded deeper, rougher, thick with emotion.

Zoe held her breath, wondering if he would explain his recent silence, or if he'd comment on her last message.

At least *I love you* hadn't frightened him away.

'It's beautiful here,' she said lamely.

'Where are you exactly?'

'I'm not sure. It's a little side street off the Old Town Square. Why?'

'I was hoping you weren't too far away.'

She laughed. 'Yeah, right. Like I'm just around the corner from Willara Downs.'

'I'm not at Willara Downs.'

'Where—?' she began, then froze as she heard the triumphant notes of a brass band. The music was coming from...

Inside her phone.

Surely she was mistaken?

No, she wasn't.

'Kent?' Zoe was so tense she was sure her skin had snapped. 'Where are you?'

'Right behind you.'

Heart thumping, she spun around.

And there he was.

On the street corner in a heavy winter coat, outlined by the bright lights from the markets.

She tried to lift a shocked hand to wave, but already Kent was coming towards her, and then, as fast as her shaky legs would allow, Zoe was stumbling over the snowy cobblestones.

Into his open arms.

She buried her face in his shoulder and he held her. She was crying, laughing and snuffling with happiness.

'What are you doing here?' she asked when she got her breath back.

'Looking for you, of course.'

'Kent, that's insane.' A huge sob burst from her. 'Oh, God, I've missed you so much.'

'And I've missed you.' Kent wiped her tears with a gloved hand. 'You wrote that you missed me on your first day here, and I jumped straight on the very next plane.'

Stunned, she pulled back to look into his face. His dearly loved, beautiful face. And in that moment she understood exactly why she loved him.

It had nothing to do with his farm, or his lovely homestead. Or his country shirts and his riding boots. She loved him for something else entirely. Something warm and powerful and steadfast and strong that she found shining in his beautiful brown eyes.

'Thank you for coming,' she said softly.

'Thank you for missing me,' he answered, kissing the tip of her nose.

Arm in arm and warmed by mulled wine and hot corn cobs, they walked through the snowy night to Zoe's hotel. Kent was insanely happy. *Insanely. Over the moon.*

They collected his backpack and went up the narrow stairs. In Zoe's room, they peeled off their gloves, hung up their woollen hats and coats, and removed their heavy, damp boots.

Zoe, looking all kinds of gorgeous in a soft crimson sweater and pale blue jeans, turned to him, her eyes shining with happy expectation.

He wanted nothing more than to scoop her in to him, but he remembered, just in time, that he had something even more important planned for this moment.

He said, with a rueful smile, 'Can you hang on a tick?'

'No, Kent, I can't.' Zoe was laughing and impatient,

rising on tiptoes to nuzzle his jaw. With her lips against his skin, she growled, 'I can't wait another second.'

OK, it was a whacky plan anyway, and Kent knew he couldn't wait either. He needed this. Now. Needed Zoe wrapped in his arms, needed her sweet mouth locked with his, needed the soft silk of her skin under his palms, needed her eager and hungry and loving…

Later…

Everything else could wait till later…

'So what was it?' Zoe asked much later as she lay with her head cradled against his bare shoulder.

Kent yawned. 'What was what?'

'Earlier tonight, when we got back here to the room, you asked me to hang on. What was that about? Were you going to show me something?'

'Yeah,' he said sleepily, and then he yawned. 'But it can wait.'

Gently, she ran her fingers over his chest. 'Poor Kent. You've flown all this way and you must be so jet-lagged.'

'Mmm.'

Kent slept, and Zoe lay awake. After the strain of the past few days, she should have been exhausted, but she was too happy and excited to close her eyes.

Kent had come to her as soon as she told him she missed him. How wonderful was that?

Faint moonlight spilled from the window across their bed and she watched him sleep and thought how amazing, how unbelievably perfect he was.

Her happiness was astonishing, as if she'd been living in a grey world that was suddenly flooded with colour.

Of course, in a deep corner of her heart there was still a niggle of disquiet. When Kent had swept her into his arms he hadn't promised love or marriage. But perhaps it was time to put her dreams aside. Time to put Rodney behind her and to take another risk. Didn't loving someone always involve a risk?

Bella had taken a huge risk when she dashed off to Far North Queensland with Damon Cavello. Kent had taken another big risk by travelling over here on the strength of a text message...

Anyway, why should she worry now simply because Kent hadn't actually told her in so many words that he loved her? He'd flown all this way to be with her, and he'd made love to her with a passion that made her blood sing.

Really. On a night like this, just having him here was enough.

Kent kissed Zoe awake. 'Morning, Sleeping Beauty. I've brought you coffee.'

To her surprise it was already past ten.

'Gosh, you're the one with jet lag. I should be bringing you coffee.'

Kent smiled and sat on the edge of the bed. 'Did you know you're at your most beautiful when you've just woken up?'

'I can't be.'

'But you are. I love the sleep-tumbled look.'

For a moment she thought he was going to say he loved her—no matter how she looked.

It doesn't matter. I don't need words.

Outside, the day was sunny, crystal clear and gleaming white, but they stayed in until lunchtime, making leisurely love. When they eventually went out, they ate food from a market stall, then took a train ride to Karlstejn Castle.

The castle was stunningly beautiful, and Zoe decided that Cinderella, Snow White and Sleeping Beauty had all spent time living within those spectacular walls at the top of a snowy mountain.

From the castle ramparts, the view was truly majestic. They could see for miles, and Zoe wondered—just briefly, as she had earlier that morning—if *this* setting might prompt Kent to tell her he'd changed, that he loved her and wanted to spend the rest of his life with her...

It didn't happen.

But that was OK. Nothing could spoil her happiness as they took the train back to Prague, or as they walked to Wenceslas Square to a café that served coffee and sensational apple strudel with home-made ice cream.

'Save room for dinner,' Kent warned her. 'I'm taking you somewhere special.'

So they walked off the strudel, then went back to their hotel to change. Kent had made reservations at the most gorgeous restaurant where the food was so divine it could easily have inspired a brand-new 'Bohemian Rhapsody'.

Over dinner they talked about Prague and what they knew of Czech history, and the whole time Kent's eyes were lit by a special light that kept Zoe's heart zinging.

All right, all right...

There was no talk of love. *But who needed words?*

Back at the hotel, Zoe took a long hot bath and told herself that she had to stop waiting for Kent to say *something*.

He was a farmer, a doer, a man of action, not words.

He'd bought her a bracelet and he'd sent her goldfish and flowers and given her a book. He'd rushed to the airport to farewell her. And he'd flown all this way from Australia. Why would he do all that if he didn't really care for her?

Just the same…tonight, she would pluck up the courage to mention her last revealing text message. She needed to know how he felt about it…

After drying herself, Zoe rubbed moisturiser all over her body, then slipped into the luxuriously thick towelling robe supplied by the hotel. She opened the bathroom door…

And gasped when she saw their room…

Candles…

Candles everywhere. Candles on the coffee table, on the bookcase, on the bedside tables, on the deep stone window sills. Candles on every available surface. Dainty, *little* candles.

Candles that looked strangely familiar.

Kent was standing in the middle of the room, watching her. In the flickering light, he sent her a shy, crooked smile. 'This was supposed to happen last night.'

'Wow.' Zoe pressed a hand to the jumping pulse in her throat. 'They look so lovely.'

The candles were more than lovely. They were gorgeous. Dazzling. The room danced and glowed with romantic light, while darkness hovered outside and white snowflakes fell soundlessly against the window pane.

Kent grinned. 'You probably recognise these little guys. I have to confess I borrowed your smart candles.'

Of course. Now she knew why they were so familiar. They were the same candles she'd planned to put in sand-filled paper bags for Bella's wedding. 'You brought all of them? All this way?'

'Yes. Four dozen smart candles in my backpack.' He smiled boyishly. 'I brought them to help me.'

Help him? Why? Zoe held her breath. Her heart began to thump.

Kent stepped closer and reached for her hands. 'I wanted to tell you how special you are, Zoe, but I wasn't sure I could convince you with words alone. The candles are my back-up.' His eyes shimmered. 'They stand for everything I love about you. They're bright and—'

'Wait,' she said. 'Please, don't rush over that bit.'

'What bit?'

'The—ah—bit you just said.'

'About loving you?'

'Yes.'

Kent smiled gorgeously. 'Darling girl, that's why I'm here.' His hands framed her face. His eyes shone. 'I love you so much. So much it kills me.'

She was so happy she was going to cry. But she still mustn't get her hopes up. She had to stay sensible. 'But—but this isn't a proposal or anything, is it?'

'It certainly is.'

Her heart almost leapt clear out of her chest. 'But you—you said—'

'I know what I said about long-term commitment, but that was before.' Kent's throat rippled and his eyes shimmered. 'Everything changed when you stepped on that plane, Zoe. I watched you walking out of my life, and it was like I was drowning all over again. Every moment I'd spent with you flashed before my eyes—from the first time we met by the road side and you had the flat tyre, and all those other times at Willara, and then in Brisbane.'

He took a deep breath. 'I've been falling for you from

the start, but I was planning the wedding to Bella, and I couldn't let myself think about you.'

Lifting her hands, Kent pressed them against his chest and she felt the thud-thudding of his heartbeats. 'I've missed you so much. And I've come to my senses at last. Of course, I want what you want, Zoe. I want your help with running the farm, and I want our own little family.'

It was too, too wonderful to take in. To Zoe's dismay, fat tears rolled down her cheeks and she had to blot them on Kent's shirtfront.

When she looked up again, his dark eyes burned with an intensity that made her tremble. 'Don't ever doubt that I love you, Zoe. You're exactly like these candles. You're beautiful and smart and you set me alight.'

'And you brought all forty-eight of them all this way to prove it.' Smiling, she snuggled closer and wound her arms around his neck. 'I do love a man of action.'

'So does that mean you'll marry me?'

Would she? Would she marry the most gorgeous farmer in the world and live in his lovely farmhouse set solidly and safely amidst spreading fields?

Would she embrace her most cherished dream?

For answer Zoe kissed him. 'Yes,' she said, and she gave him another kiss. 'Yes, please, I'd love to marry you.' Then she kissed him again while forty-eight candles glowed warmly in the midwinter night.

* * * * *

Mills & Boon® Hard Back

October 2011

ROMANCE

HISTORICAL

MEDICAL ROMANCE™

Mills & Boon® Large Print

October 2011

ROMANCE

Passion and the Prince	Penny Jordan
For Duty's Sake	Lucy Monroe
Alessandro's Prize	Helen Bianchin
Mr and Mischief	Kate Hewitt
Her Desert Prince	Rebecca Winters
The Boss's Surprise Son	Teresa Carpenter
Ordinary Girl in a Tiara	Jessica Hart
Tempted by Trouble	Liz Fielding

HISTORICAL

Secret Life of a Scandalous Debutante	Bronwyn Scott
One Illicit Night	Sophia James
The Governess and the Sheikh	Marguerite Kaye
Pirate's Daughter, Rebel Wife	June Francis

MEDICAL ROMANCE™

Taming Dr Tempest	Meredith Webber
The Doctor and the Debutante	Anne Fraser
The Honourable Maverick	Alison Roberts
The Unsung Hero	Alison Roberts
St Piran's: The Fireman and Nurse Loveday	Kate Hardy
From Brooding Boss to Adoring Dad	Dianne Drake

ROMANCE

The Power of Vasilii	Penny Jordan
The Real Rio D'Aquila	Sandra Marton
A Shameful Consequence	Carol Marinelli
A Dangerous Infatuation	Chantelle Shaw
Kholodov's Last Mistress	Kate Hewitt
His Christmas Acquisition	Cathy Williams
The Argentine's Price	Maisey Yates
Captive but Forbidden	Lynn Raye Harris
On the First Night of Christmas...	Heidi Rice
The Power and the Glory	Kimberly Lang
How a Cowboy Stole Her Heart	Donna Alward
Tall, Dark, Texas Ranger	Patricia Thayer
The Secretary's Secret	Michelle Douglas
Rodeo Daddy	Soraya Lane
The Boy is Back in Town	Nina Harrington
Confessions of a Girl-Next-Door	Jackie Braun
Mistletoe, Midwife...Miracle Baby	Anne Fraser
Dynamite Doc or Christmas Dad?	Marion Lennox

HISTORICAL

The Lady Confesses	Carole Mortimer
The Dangerous Lord Darrington	Sarah Mallory
The Unconventional Maiden	June Francis
Her Battle-Scarred Knight	Meriel Fuller

MEDICAL ROMANCE™

The Child Who Rescued Christmas	Jessica Matthews
Firefighter With A Frozen Heart	Dianne Drake
How to Save a Marriage in a Million	Leonie Knight
Swallowbrook's Winter Bride	Abigail Gordon